"I have a gift for you," Bill said, holding out a velvet box

Lila propped herself up on the rumpled pillows and opened the little box. A diamond solitaire. She glanced up at Bill, her mouth suddenly dry.

"I know what we said—no strings attached— but, Lila, this is the only solution."

"I don't see how this solves anything," she stammered, overwhelmed by Bill's proposal. "There's so much we haven't talked about. Like the eighty miles between us."

Bill sat on the bed, a knot in his gut. This wasn't going according to plan. "I want you to sell your business and move in with me."

With a shaking hand she closed the box and placed it on the sheet between them. "Before I met you, I had created happiness for myself. Without depending on a man to be happy." Getting out of bed, she hastily reached for her clothes. "I don't intend to change that!"

"But we love each other!" Bill protested.

"Does that mean we have to give away chunks of ourselves in the process? If so, a goodbye is in order." She stalked from the room without looking back.

Dear Reader,

I wonder if love really is "more comfortable" the
second time around. First-time lovers adapt more
easily to each other's quirks, I think, than people
who, because they've been doing it that way for
years, already know how they want their coffee
brewed and their toothpaste squeezed.

I felt bringing together two such full-fledged adults
with their life-styles firmly in place would create a
fascinatingly complex love affair. I was right. Bill
and Lila aren't about to mold themselves to suit
someone else, not even in the face of their
compelling attraction for each other. Fortunately
they discover a solution that doesn't compromise
their individuality, a solution I hope you'll find fun
and a little bit inspiring. Happy reading!

Sincerely,

Vicki Lewis Thompson

Your Place or Mine

VICKI LEWIS THOMPSON

Harlequin Books

TORONTO • NEW YORK • LONDON
AMSTERDAM • PARIS • SYDNEY • HAMBURG
STOCKHOLM • ATHENS • TOKYO • MILAN

Published April 1991

ISBN 0-373-25444-X

YOUR PLACE OR MINE

1

"THIS IS THE ULTIMATE seasickness test," Lila whispered to her friend Penny as the cruise ship heaved through another wave and the silverware rattled. Storm or no storm, the crew was serving the first formal dinner of the trip. At Lila and Penny's table vichyssoise lapped at the edges of six bowls and wine rippled in six goblets.

"We'll be fine," Penny whispered back. "It'll blow over in no time."

"There are whitecaps in my soup," Lila grumbled, just as the wood-paneled dining room tilted and the entire table service slid toward her.

"Grab that stuff!" a man at their table shouted over the din. Everyone in the circle obeyed.

Once the ship had leveled out, Lila made a clockwise damage check. Her friend Penny wore vichyssoise down the front of her sequined blouse. Next to Penny a newlywed couple had been baptized with red wine. On their left the handsome gray-haired devil who had ordered everyone to react had a sportcoat sleeve decorated with soup. Beside him his college-age son mopped his tie.

Lila's red silk suit alone remained untouched. "Thank you all very much," she said, trying to keep a straight face.

"It was nothing," said the father with a grin.

His smile and compelling blue gaze jolted Lila with unexpected force. She'd always had a soft spot for amused gallantry, but something more than his good sportsmanship had initiated that tickle of desire in her stomach. "I think you should all send me your cleaning bills," she said, lingering over the sparkle of interest in the stranger's eyes.

"I'd say it's the ship's responsibility, not yours," he said, his tone smoother than bourbon.

Penny's nudge brought Lila to her senses and she dropped her gaze. "Maybe so." She was treading on dangerous ground by exchanging glances with this man. Penny had claimed him from the moment they'd noticed him striding up the gangplank in L.A. His lean good looks burnished with a California tan had prompted Penny to remark that he looked like Paul Newman. That was enough to satisfy her fantasies. Finding him seated at their table with no wedding band on his left hand and no wife in sight had been the answer to Penny's prayers for an exciting cruise.

"Whoops," the new husband said, steadying his soup. "Here we go again."

"Is this worth it?" asked his bride as everyone grabbed for the dishes once more. "I don't feel like eating, anyway, with the boat pitching around like this."

"*Ship*, dear. Ship," her husband corrected. "You look a little pale, sweetheart."

"Who wouldn't with red wine spilled all over that white eyelet dress?" Penny commented, wetting a napkin to dab at the soup congealing on her sequins. "I'd sponge that stuff off, honey, before it stains."

The bride glanced down at her wine-spattered dress. When the floor began tipping again, she swallowed and gripped her husband's arm. "Eddie, let's go back to the cabin."

"You bet, sweetheart." Eddie leaped to his feet and helped her with her chair.

"They may have the right idea," said the Paul Newman look-alike.

"Oh, they're newlyweds," Penny said, winking at him. "Being seasick was probably an excuse to be alone. We may not see them again the whole trip."

The ship pitched again, but not enough to cause anymore accidents at the table. Lila grimaced and leaned toward Penny. "This isn't my idea of fun, Pen. How're you doing?"

"Just dandy," Penny said, maintaining a camera-ready smile.

"You're green as a toad."

"Thanks," Penny said, her smile fixed. "You're looking lovely tonight, too." Then she turned her attention to the man seated across from her. "We won't let a little storm at sea bother us, will we, Bill?"

Lila had forgotten that the man's name was Bill, but obviously Penny had stored the information permanently when they'd all introduced themselves by first names at the beginning of the dinner.

Bill looked uncertain and glanced at his son. "What do you think, Jason? Want to stick it out?"

"I don't know. Some trip, huh, Dad? If our luck keeps up like this, we can expect Montezuma's revenge in Mexico."

"I'm sure everything will be fine," Bill assured him in the rich baritone that Lila was beginning to enjoy far too much.

Jason groaned. "Damn, they're bringing more food." He looked away as a waiter staggered by on the unsteady floor with a tray of heaping plates.

As the waiter passed their table the aroma of the food he was carrying made Lila's stomach churn. "Lots of people are bailing out," she said, checking around the dining room.

"Not me," maintained Penny. "I'm on this cruise to have a good time, to eat, drink and be merry." She took a gulp of wine. "Four days and three nights isn't very long, and I plan to make the most of it."

Jason blanched and pushed back his chair. "Hey, Dad, you can be macho about this if you want, but I'm outa here. If you want me, I'll be in my cabin until this tub settles down."

"If I leave, I'm heading for the deck," Bill said. "I'd feel better if I could see the coastline, if it's not too dark out there, that is."

Penny took another hefty swallow of wine. "My goodness, such party poopers," she said. "I'm feeling just—" The floor shifted beneath them and she gripped the table. "Then again, maybe a turn around the deck would be nice."

"That's my choice," Lila said, standing unsteadily. "Fresh air is my only hope. Let's go, Pen. This is ridiculous."

Penny glanced from Lila to Bill. "Care to join us on deck, Bill?" she asked.

Lila couldn't believe Penny's persistence. Even though she was seasick, Penny hung in there, hoping to snag the interest of this apparently unattached man. The ship rocked again.

"Sure," Bill said. "Lead the way."

They lurched between the tables on their way out and grabbed the handrails as they climbed the stairs to the upper deck.

"Remember *The Poseidon Adventure*?" Bill asked as they staggered out onto the covered promenade.

"Stop that." Penny tied a scarf over her ash-blond hair. "This ship is not going to sink."

"I don't remember this scene in the cruise brochure," Lila said, as she and Bill stumbled toward the railing.

The storm had darkened the sky, but there was enough light to make out the California coast as a faint slash on the horizon. Rain and salt spray spat at them.

"The seawater won't be good for that red silk, either," Bill commented as he braced himself beside her and his coat brushed her arm.

She had the insane urge to hurl herself into the safety of his arms and hold on until the ship stopped pitching. Instinct told her she'd be welcomed. Instead, Lila dug the heels of her red satin pumps into the rubber tread covering the deck, gripped the rail, and chose to talk about laundry—a dull, passionless subject if ever there was one. "I hate to admit this, after the way everyone sacrificed their clothes to save mine, but this suit is made of washable silk. I could easily rinse it out in the sink."

Penny inserted herself between them at the railing. "Which is more than I can say for these sequins," she muttered.

Lila made room for her friend. Just as well Penny should separate them, Lila thought. The possibility of accidental contact with Bill had created a dangerous feeling of excitement she hadn't experienced in years. Penny wanted this Bill person, and no matter how his blue eyes and seductive voice made Lila feel, romance didn't fit into her life right now. "I recommend deep breathing," she said. "At least, that helps me."

"It sounds as if you've had experience with seasickness before," Bill commented as the ship knifed through another heavy wave.

"My ex-husband owned a small cabin cruiser," Lila replied. *One more big-ticket item he couldn't afford.*

Penny moved closer to Bill. "My late husband wasn't into boats at all. I've always wanted to take a cruise, so this is the realization of a dream for me. Oh, excuse me, did I bump into you? It's hard to stay steady on this deck."

"No kidding," Bill agreed as the horizon seesawed in front of them. "Ever see *Raise the Titanic*?"

"Bill, that's quite enough. Everything will be lovely once the storm's over," Penny insisted. "Excuse me again. My, but I can't seem to stand upright."

Lila recognized the ploy. Penny was angling for a comforting male arm tucked around her waist, but Bill didn't seem to want to play the game. Instead, he moved over to give Penny more room.

"Just wait until the moon comes out," Penny said. "It'll be so romantic. It's a shame your wife couldn't make it, Bill."

Lila stared at her friend in amazement. Penny was determined to nail down this man's eligibility, even under the onslaught of a rough ride and queasy stomachs.

Bill gave Penny a calculating glance. "Yes, it is a shame," he said, and put more distance between them.

Penny seemed startled. No wonder, Lila thought—they'd both assumed he was single. Lila couldn't imagine why a married man would be alone on a cruise with his son, but whatever the reason, his answer would bring down the curtain on Penny's flirting. Her moral code would never allow her to become involved with somebody else's husband.

Penny looked at Lila with a pout of disappointment and shrugged. "You know, the fresh air has helped me," she said. "I think I'll go below, after all. Maybe I can still salvage these sequins."

"I'll be along shortly," Lila said, deciding to give this stranger a piece of her mind once Penny moved out of earshot. She felt sorry for her friend. From the moment they'd left the dock, Penny's hopes had been pinned on this man with his strong profile and lean, tanned physique. Judging from the gray in his hair and the lines of experience on his face, he was in his mid to late forties, the perfect age for Penny. Lila watched Penny teeter across the deck toward the doorway.

"Your friend needs to inject some subtlety into her act," Bill said, closing the gap between them at the railing. "She'll never find a husband if she doesn't soften that edge of desperation."

Lila stiffened. "I beg your pardon?"

"Sorry. I guess that was a little blunt, but honestly, I've had it up to here with women who can't carry on a decent conversation until they find out if I'm married."

"Oh, really?" Lila glared at him as her loyalty to Penny fueled her anger. "It must be dreadful being so sought after, especially when you're not even free." Privately she saw merit in his objection to Penny's approach, but Penny had been her best friend for thirty years. "Frankly, I think you're asking for it by traveling without your wife, not wearing a wedding band, taking a cruise where lots of single women—"

"Hold it. Let me clear up a misconception. This cruise was Jason's idea—not mine—as a college graduation present. I would have been just as happy with a fishing trip, but Jason had this thing about a cruise, and he wanted me along. I'm here because it's a chance to spend time with the kid before he heads east for his first serious job."

"So what about your wife?" Lila shot back, incensed. "Doesn't she deserve to spend some time with Jason, too? And come to think of it, what sort of man would leave his wife at home to slave away while he sailed into the sunset on a ship full of eligible women?"

He glanced at her before returning his attention to the horizon. "My wife died six years ago."

"Died?" Lila spun around to face him, indignation overriding caution. "Then why did you lie to my friend, Mr. Bill Whatever-your-name-is? Just tell me that!" she demanded, and promptly was thrown toward him as the ship dived into another wave.

He reacted quickly, turning in time to catch her elbows and keep her from falling. "Steady," he murmured.

She clutched his arms for support, and as in her earlier fantasy, support was there. The flex of his muscles and a whiff of after-shave coaxed her to look into his eyes. The invitation in his gaze nearly snared her, but just in time she remembered Penny and stepped away from him. "Sorry. And thanks," she muttered, gripping the railing and staring out at the horizon while she patched together her dignity and quieted her thumping heart. "I still want to know why you lied to Penny."

"I didn't lie," he said in a low rumble that caused her to glance back at him. He regarded her with a gaze hardened by her subtle rejection. "She mentioned it was a shame my wife couldn't be here, and I agreed. It is a shame."

Well, he had pride, Lila thought, taking a steadying breath. "It's not much different," she said, challenging his bold stare. "You still deliberately misled her."

"Yes, I did that," he said, his tone more intense. "Because your friend Penny had *manhunter* written all over her. I am sick to death of women who don't care a thing about me, really, except that I'll help pay the bills, and fix the leaky kitchen faucet or the flat tire, and keep the boogeyman away."

Lila's grip on the railing tightened. "That's a rotten assumption to make so quickly. You don't know that Penny's that kind of woman. And I happen to know she's certainly not," she added forcefully.

"Okay. You're her friend, so I suppose you'd know. But everything else aside, she's out to get herself a husband as soon as possible, right?"

Lila seethed at his arrogance. She'd take him down a peg before she left this deck. "What if she is? She's no different from a hundred men I've met in the past five years. You talk about leaky faucets? All men want from a wife is clean socks and clean sex."

Bill gazed at her in bewilderment for a moment, and then he laughed.

His good humor took her aback, but she attempted to turn it to her advantage. "See? You're laughing because it's true."

"I'm laughing because it's funny. I like that line— *clean socks and clean sex.*"

"And usually in that order, too," she said, struggling to keep a straight face despite his broad grin.

He sobered and looked at her with a glint in his eyes. "Oh, really? What type of nerd do you hang out with?"

She tried to think of a snappy reply. None came. Instead, meeting the challenge in his gaze, she felt anger being replaced by desire yet again. Whatever type of male she was used to, this man clearly set himself apart and deliberately aroused her curiosity. She'd have to be careful. "The point is, most men expect women to be unpaid domestic help. Which is why I don't intend to fill that role ever again."

"Ever?" Bill's eyebrow lifted. "That's an unusual statement coming from a woman."

"You think so? Maybe you haven't been listening. Welcome to the modern age, my friend. I know lots of women who see marriage as a sweet deal for the guy and lots of menial work for the woman. Consequently, they've decided not to marry—or remarry, for that matter."

"A sweet deal for men? Then how come they usually die off first and the women inherit all their hard-earned money? Most of the wealth in this country is in the hands of women, and lots of them are widows."

"And most of that money is still controlled by men," Lila shot back, "—investment bankers, attorneys, even sons and grandsons."

"I'll bet your friend Penny isn't in that category."

"No, fortunately. *She's* in charge of her money."

"Which was earned by her late husband?"

"Yes," Lila said testily, "while Penny took care of his every need."

"I have the feeling you don't quite approve."

She ignored his sarcasm. "It's okay for Penny because it's what she wanted, still wants. She loves having someone to take care of, someone depending on her."

The ship's rocking eased off. Bill leaned against the railing and shoved one hand into his slacks pocket. "I don't understand."

"What don't you understand?" Lila wondered if he had any idea the picture he made lounging there, his tie loosened, his hair ruffled by the wind. If Penny hadn't—but no. No. Lila didn't want a lover now.

"If all of us opportunistic guys are out there just waiting to take advantage of a good-hearted woman like Penny," Bill continued, "why hasn't she landed one of us yet?"

Lila hesitated. "Well . . . Penny also has a stiff requirement about . . . never mind."

"What? Come on. You can't leave it like that. Religion? Education? Social activism?"

"Bodies."

Bill smiled. "Bodies?"

"Yes." Lila glanced away from him. She'd caught herself focusing on the buttons of his shirt and longing to undo at least one, maybe two. "Lots of men your age have let themselves run to flab. Penny only dates men who have nice physiques." Concentrating on the choppy waves illuminated by the ship's lights, she raced on. "She says that if she's going to take care of a man, the only thing she demands in exchange is a nice view."

Bill chuckled. "Pretty choosy, isn't she?"

"Is she?" Lila took refuge in their former debate as she turned back to him. "I've noticed that men apply that criterion all the time. Why shouldn't a woman?"

"Do you?"

"No." And consequently she hadn't been physically attracted to the men she'd dated, she thought. Her four-alarm reaction to Bill was educational.

"I see." He surveyed her with amusement. "Then any old flabby guy will do for you?"

"That's not what I meant. I meant that I don't apply any criteria at the moment. I'm just not interested, period."

"Hmm."

He wasn't contradicting her, but Lila didn't think he believed her for a minute. A man like Bill knew when a woman was interested, despite what she said to the contrary.

"You must have met some Neanderthals since your divorce," he said. "How long's it been?"

"I don't think that's relevant."

"I guess not. You're still mad at the world, I can tell that much."

"Perhaps I am." She wished he'd stop making such uncomfortably accurate assessments. "I wouldn't expect a man, especially one as sought-after as you, to understand."

"You're right. I don't understand why someone like you has given up on men. How old are you? Hell, I bet you're barely forty."

"It's not important," she said, pleased that he'd underestimated her age by five years.

"No, it's not. What is important is that you've lived long enough, and loved long enough, to have far more fun in bed than a twenty-five-year-old. And you're wasting the best years of your life."

Her pulse raced. "Typical male assumption," she retorted, losing the battle to stay calm. "You think sex is everything."

"That's a step up from socks." His blue gaze assessed her, beckoned, made promises.

Her restraint began to slip. If he forced the issue, if he tried to kiss her . . . She edged away, ready to make her escape. This exchange was becoming far too dangerous. "Listen, Bill, I'd better—"

"Wait. Before you go, I want you to hear this. I think you're a very sexy, if slightly bitter, woman."

"Bill, don't—"

"I happen to like brunette coloring, and I've been admiring those huge brown eyes all evening," he continued, ignoring her attempt to interrupt him. "Despite what you've said, there's something lurking in those eyes, Lila, something wild. You may not realize how that look turns men on, but I assure you, it has a powerful effect."

"Completely unintentional." She couldn't tell him that *he* was responsible for that look.

"Extremely provocative."

Lila took a step backward, all the while fighting the temptation to run into his arms, into the ecstasy that lured her.

"You should also know that I don't give a damn about clean socks."

She gazed into his blue eyes and shivered.

"Cold?" he said, noticing her slight trembling.

"Yes," she lied.

"No wonder, with only that thin silk between you and the elements. Take my coat," he said, starting to strip it off.

"No!" she cried, backing away from him, from his chivalrous offer, from a temptation too hot to handle. "I mean, no thank you."

He paused and shrugged back into the coat. "What's the matter, Lila?" he asked softly. "Did I put a crack in that feminist armor you're wearing?"

"I don't know what you're talking about."

"The hell you don't."

"I really should be going. Penny will wonder where I am." She glanced at the horizon. "The storm's almost over."

"You share a cabin with Penny?"

"Yes." Lila realized that she'd have to go back there and explain Bill's actual marital status to Penny. A friend wouldn't keep that information to herself. Then she ought to convince Penny that Bill was a lost cause.

Furthermore, she'd have to explain all that without giving any indication that Bill was attracted to *her*, instead—an attraction that must come to nothing. A romance with him would be a slap in the face to Penny. After all, she'd wanted him first. Besides, Lila was on this cruise to rest; she was not here to add another complication to her already hectic life. Despite the crazy longings Bill inspired, she believed what she'd told Bill: men were more trouble than they were worth.

"I'd like to see you again," Bill said.

"You will. We've been assigned to the same table for all our meals on this cruise."

"That's not what I meant."

"I know."

"By the way, if all this talk about avoiding men is true, what are you doing on this cruise, looking so single and available?"

"I—"

"Not to mention that red silk number showing off your womanly figure, which I've restrained myself from commenting upon. Aren't you being a little unfair and misleading?"

Lila warmed with sensual awareness as she realized that the wind must have pushed the flimsy material of her dress against her body, outlining its every curve. She'd been so absorbed in their argument that she hadn't noticed . . . but he had. "I'm keeping Penny company," she said, folding her arms over her chest and edging away, "and relaxing."

"Then why don't you look relaxed?"

"Because I've allowed this conversation to go on far too long."

"Lila, I—darn it, I'm intrigued by a woman who's running away for a change. I'll admit that much."

"Then I guess you'll have to stay intrigued. Good night, Bill." She turned and hurried away, her thoughts whirling. Penny would be crushed if she realized what had happened after she'd left—that Bill had all but propositioned her best friend. But Lila hadn't meant that to happen, and it would end here; she wouldn't allow anything to develop.

She took the stairway instead of the elevator down to their cabin, giving herself more time to prepare what she'd say to her roommate. Surely there were other men on this ship who would welcome a woman like Penny. Lila knew there were, of course, but the added requirement that they be built like a *Playgirl* centerfold didn't help matters.

Penny hadn't given herself enough time to look, Lila decided. She'd focused on Bill immediately, and once they'd arrived at dinner and discovered him sitting there with his son, Penny had made her choice. Well, she'd have to unmake it, and Lila would help her.

Lila found Penny kneeling by the bed in her bra and slip while she ironed a new outfit. Her sequined blouse hung dripping in the shower.

"Is the blouse salvageable?" Lila asked, peering into the tiny cubicle of a bathroom.

"Oh, sure." Penny glanced up from her task. "You know me, the laundry champ of La Jolla. Can you beat that news about old Bill? I'd hate to be his wife, if he won't even take her with him on a cruise with their son."

Lila sat on her twin bed at a right angle from Penny's and took off her satin pumps. "I learned a bit more about Bill after you left," she said slowly. "His wife's dead, Penny."

"Dead?" Penny tipped up the travel iron and rested it on a folded towel. "The poor man! Oh, Lila, I feel just awful, bringing up such a sensitive subject. Did he come on this cruise to forget?"

"I hardly think so. She died six years ago."

"Six years?" Penny looked confused. "It must still hurt a lot if he can't talk about it. I'll have to apologize, of course. I hope you told him that I don't usually trample all over people's feelings, but when he was here with just his son, I naturally assumed—"

"Pen, save your sympathy," Lila said, massaging her instep. "The man deliberately let you think he had a wife. He avoids all women who seem to be looking for a husband."

"Oh, for heaven's sake!" With a jerk Penny unplugged the iron. "I've never heard such nonsense.

What did he think I planned to do, drag him in front of the captain for a ceremony tonight?"

Lila smiled. "Just about. Face facts. You were rather obvious."

"I was only acting friendly," Penny protested, "but I can see I'll have to alter my approach if he's so gun-shy."

"Alter? I think you'd better *abandon* your approach. Trust me, this Bill character is not for you."

Penny stood and reached for the shimmering gold dress she'd been pressing. "Are you kidding? Did you notice the shoulders on that man? Lila, bodies like that don't come along every day, especially in our age bracket."

"Haven't you been listening? He has no interest in remarrying. None. Zip. He's a lost cause."

"Lots of men say that." Penny pulled the dress over her head. "It's not true," she added, her voice muffled by the material.

Lila rolled her eyes toward the ceiling. "Don't go after him, Penny," she said. "I'm warning you, he'll run like crazy. He's got you pegged as a lady with marriage on her mind. I'm sure there are plenty of other eligible men on this ship who don't have his particular hang-up about matrimony."

"Yes," agreed Penny, poking her head through the neck of the dress, "but do they have pecs like Bill's?"

"I don't know," Lila sighed. "We'll look."

"We can do that, but I doubt if we'll find anyone to compare with him." She reached for her hairbrush. "Are you coming down to the casino with me?"

"I don't know. I'm feeling a little—"

"Lila, you know how we've looked forward to playing the slot machines." She gestured with her brush. "Besides, it's a great way to meet men."

I've already met one too many, Lila thought. "Penny, I told you right from the start that I'm here to rest, not to meet men."

"I know, but I figured once we sailed, you'd loosen up and have some fun."

"Resting will be loads of fun." As if to demonstrate, Lila stretched out on the bed and closed her eyes. "For these few days I intend to try to forget the pressures of the office, and the fact that my daughter has left her husband and moved in with me, bringing her ten-month-old baby boy along with her, and that my other daughter is flunking out of college." She opened one eye. "Don't talk to me about romance, Penny. I'm not up to it."

"Oh, Lila." Penny chuckled. "What am I going to do with you, girl? At least indulge in some harmless flirting on this trip. What could it hurt?"

"My already endangered peace of mind." Lila remembered the way Bill had looked at her. No. she wouldn't think about that again.

"Anyway," Penny said, "we're wasting time debating the subject. Put on some fresh makeup and come down to the casino with me. We'll survey the entire crop of men. I'll guarantee none will measure up to Bill, but maybe we can find someone for you."

"Read my lips. I don't want someone."

"Okay, then come for the excitement of a little innocent gambling. And if we can see Bill, I'll do what I can to repair the damage I've done."

Lila sat up. "Penny, please listen. He—"

"He's a man," Penny interrupted. "I know that territory backward and forward. I'll bring him around, and now that I've found out there's no wife waiting on shore, I'm free to try anything I want."

Lila groaned and went into the bathroom to reapply her makeup. She'd tried to warn Penny away, but her friend wouldn't listen. Lila had one more argument to make to Penny, but she couldn't bring herself to use it.

If Lila recounted the whole conversation on deck, including the parts in which Bill made his preference for Lila known, Penny would back off immediately. But her feelings would be hurt and she might even feel betrayed by her best friend, and Lila wanted to avoid all that if possible.

Maybe Penny would be able to successfully win Bill over, now that she knew how skittish he was. Penny was a striking woman, with generous breasts and a firm figure. More importantly, she had a kind nature, a quick wit, and her own income. In Lila's opinion, Bill was a fool to reject her. And yet, the thought of Penny and Bill together made Lila feel vaguely uneasy. *Damn.* She couldn't afford to want him for herself. She just couldn't.

2

LILA AND PENNY STOOD at the entrance to the smoky casino and listened to human noise piled on top of mechanical noise. On one side of the room the bleep of slot machines mingled with the jangle of coins into metal trays whenever someone hit a jackpot. From the other side came the crackle of new cards, the click of the roulette wheel and the clatter of dice.

"Loud, huh?" Penny commented.

Lila nodded as her gaze swept the room. He wasn't there. Gradually her rapid heartbeat slowed.

"Darn, I don't see Bill." Penny said. "Do you? He's tall enough that you'd think we'd notice him, even in this mob."

"He's not here," Lila said.

"What a bummer."

Lila said nothing. She shouldn't be sorry that Bill wasn't in the room, but she was.

"Maybe we should try the lounge," Penny said.

Lila started to agree but caught herself. She wanted to find Penny a substitute for Bill, not chase all over the ship trying to locate him. "Let's gamble for a while," she suggested, and lowered her voice. "If you'll open your eyes, you'll notice there are several attractive, seemingly unattached men in this room."

"Hah. I don't see anyone who compares with Bill."

Neither did Lila, but she didn't say so. "Nonsense. That man with the mustache, the one playing the poker slots, looks very nice and very lonesome."

"And very overweight. From the size of him, I'll bet he played football in high school and eats as if he still did."

"So what? You can put him on a diet. Honestly, Pen, I think you're cheating yourself out of some potentially sweet guys by insisting they have great bodies." Lila headed for the change window. "Come on, let's get some quarters."

"It's my right to insist on great bodies," Penny announced, edging through the crowd after Lila.

"Maybe we should discuss this later?" Lila suggested out of the corner of her mouth as they reached their destination.

"Don't worry. Nobody's paying attention. Do you remember high school, when I was a little pudgy and you were flat as a board?"

Lila was grateful the cashier was female. "I remember," she said, exchanging some bills for three rolls of quarters.

"Back then, the popular jocks wouldn't even talk to us because we weren't built right," Penny said, scooping up her rolls of quarters. "Ten to one your lonely man with the mustache was one of those uppity guys thirty years ago. Come on, Lila, you know exactly what I'm talking about. Doesn't he fit the aging jock stereotype?"

Lila glanced back at the man. "From here, maybe, but you're not giving him much of a chance, making snap judgments like that."

"Nobody gave us much of a chance in high school, either."

Lila noted the determined set of her friend's chin, the resolve in her gray eyes. "My goodness, Penny. I didn't realize it had bothered you so much."

"Didn't it bother you?"

"Yeah, I guess," Lila admitted. "But I never plotted revenge."

"I did. It's my turn to demand a firm body. Which reminds me, let's forget this gambling stuff. I'd rather hunt for Bill."

"Pen, give it up." Even after all their years of friendship, Lila was still impressed with the way Penny hung onto an idea. But Lila had to shake her loose from this one. "We have our quarters. Let's play until they're gone."

Penny groaned. "Knowing you, that could be all night. Remember Vegas? All you wanted was one roll of quarters that time, and you nursed them for six hours!"

"I'll play faster. I'll put in two quarters at a time."

"Two? How about five?"

"A dollar twenty-five each game?"

"Yeah," Penny said, nudging her in the ribs with her elbow. "Live on the edge."

"Okay. Five at a time."

"Good girl."

As they settled onto stools in front of neighboring poker slot machines, Lila peeled the end from her roll and carefully counted out five quarters.

"For Pete's sake, Lila, just spill them all into the tray," Penny said, cracking her roll open and demonstrating the technique.

Lila wrinkled her nose but obediently did what she was told.

"I'll get you loosened up yet, honey," Penny chided, and began to feed quarters into the slot.

Lila punched the buttons of her machine, but her mind wasn't on the game. She was thinking that Penny didn't really expect her to loosen up, or even want her to; that was the unspoken pact of their friendship. Penny counted on Lila to be steady, while she took the risks. Lila had never questioned that distribution of roles before, but tonight, for the first time, she felt a twinge of resentment.

She ticked off the familiar phrases as she pushed quarters into the slot. Lila the sensible one. Lila the rock. Lila the prude. Lila the—all at once her machine erupted, flashing lights and clanging bells, and she stared in disbelief at the row of cards displayed across her machine—ace, king, queen, jack, and ten of hearts.

"What? What happened?" Penny shouted, leaping from her stool. "Lila! You have a royal flush! Attendant! We need an attendant at this machine!"

Lila stood in a daze as several people gathered around to see the perfect hand. Someone bustled over with a key to silence the bells and hand Lila a voucher for her winnings.

"I can't believe it!" Penny exclaimed, hugging her. "You, of all people, winning the big jackpot. Good thing I told you to put in five quarters, huh?"

"Yeah," Lila said, still adjusting to the shock. "I don't think I've ever won anything in my life."

From behind them came a familiar male voice. "Congratulations."

At the sound of Bill's comment, Lila froze. Her first reaction was excitement; her second was fear, both for herself and for Penny. *Oh, Penny,* she thought, *don't make a fool of yourself.*

Penny spun around to face him. "Bill!" she cried. "What perfect timing. This deserves a celebration, don't you think?"

"Sure," he said easily. "How about a drink in the lounge?"

"We'd love to," Penny said immediately. "Wouldn't we, Lila?"

Lila turned slowly and gazed into Bill's eyes. Damn. Her heart was racing and her palms were damp. She'd managed to become attracted to this entirely inappropriate man, this man Penny wanted, this man for whom Lila had no space in her life. "I appreciate the thought, but I'm really pretty tired. Thanks, anyway."

Penny grabbed her arm. "Would you excuse us an eensy moment, Bill?" she asked, before dragging Lila through the crowd and out of earshot. "Are you crazy?" she whispered. "He just asked us for a drink, this marriage-shy person you say would run from me like a scalded dog. It's true he asked us both, but I know you'll be a dear and bow out after a little while."

"Penny, it's no good, I tell you," Lila said, desperate to get out of the situation. "If you want to celebrate, fine. After we're rid of Bill, you and I can go up to the lounge and have a wonderful time. But believe me, you don't want him around."

"I most certainly do!"

"Then you go have a drink with him."

"He didn't ask just me, he asked both of us, and you're the excuse, because you won this jackpot. Lila

Kedge, if you won't go for this drink, and give me a chance to fix my image with this dreamboat, I'll never forgive you."

"Penny—"

"I mean it, Lila."

"Darn it, Pen." Lila's head began to ache. "All right. One drink. You go tell him. I'll get the money."

Penny squeezed her arm. "Thanks. I know you don't believe I can bring this man to heel, but just wait. There's dancing in the lounge, and I'm a very seductive dancer."

Lila turned back to her. "I'd forgotten about the dancing. Please, Penny, I don't think—"

"Don't worry. Leave everything to me. Go get your loot, moneybags."

Not long afterward they were seated, by Penny's request, at a table next to the dance floor. In short order, drinks were in front of them, but to Lila's relief, the band was on break.

"Can you believe that jackpot?" Penny asked, raising her glass. "Here's to you, toots."

"To Lila," Bill said, raising his glass and focusing on her with an amused expression. Then he took a drink and put down the glass. "Tell me, do you gamble very often?"

"She's only been to Vegas once, and that was with me," Penny answered for her. "I love it, though. Lila has fun, too, when I can convince her to try to. Thank goodness I practically forced her to play five quarters that game."

Bill smiled at Lila. "Conservative, are you?"

"Absolutely," Lila said, aware that the label didn't fit as comfortably as it once had. "Penny's the adventurous one. I usually play the poker slots one quarter at a time. I've even been known to pick the nickel machines and play one nickle at a time. Pretty tame, huh?" *Pretty boring*, she realized. Oh well. She was trying to turn Bill off, right?

"Maybe you just like to prolong the fun," Bill said. Under the table his knee touched hers so briefly it could have been accidental. Lila didn't think it was. "Nothing wrong with that," he added.

Lila flushed. She might be reading more into his remark than he'd intended, but she didn't meet his gaze, afraid of what she'd find there.

"Well, I like excitement," Penny said. "Oh, good. The band's here."

"So they are." Bill pushed back his chair. "Excuse me a minute. I'm going to request a song."

Waiting until he was far enough away not to hear, Penny leaned toward Lila. "He's requesting a song!" she whispered. "Doesn't that prove he's romantic?"

"Not necessarily. He could be requesting 'The Peppermint Twist' for all you know."

"I doubt it," Penny murmured. "I'm a little worried that he's somewhat attracted to you, but since I know you don't care about him, I can get around that."

Lila said nothing and sipped her drink.

"You're not interested, are you?" Penny asked. "I mean, after all that talk about wanting to rest . . ."

"Heavens, no, I'm not interested," Lila said, knowing that was what Penny wanted to hear. "But I don't think he's a good prospect for you, either. He'll never settle for the white picket fence routine."

"I don't know why you're so sure. You only talked with him for a little while. Besides, men are always saying such things. Anyway, here he comes. Watch this." Penny put on her most beguiling smile when Bill sat down again. "You know, all my life I've pictured how glamourous I'd feel gliding across the dance floor during a cruise. Be a darling, Bill, and help me fulfill that fantasy, would you?"

"Sure thing," Bill said. "Right after this first number. I requested it in Lila's honor. I told the bandleader that the brunette in red just won a big jackpot in the casino."

"That really wasn't necessary," Lila said quickly, with a thrill of terror mixed with a rush of excitement. Hadn't she known he'd do something like this? "I'm not a very good—"

"Ladies and gentlemen," announced the band leader, "this next number is dedicated to the lovely lady in red who managed a royal flush in the casino tonight and walked away with a sizable jackpot. Let's welcome her and her partner out on the floor with a little round of applause."

As the scattered crowd clapped politely, Bill stood and held out his hand. "Lila?"

She glared at him. "I am so embarrassed."

"It'll be worse if you don't come out and dance with me. Everybody's looking."

"Oh, go on, Lila," Penny said, giving her a little push. "It won't hurt you."

Lila realized she had no choice. She stood up as the band played the first bars of "It's All in the Game."

"Clever," she said, taking Bill's hand and moving into his arms.

"Which part?" he said, holding her close.

She tried to put some comfortable distance between them, but his grip remained firm. "I'm warning you, I'm going back to the cabin right after this dance."

"I figured you might, but I wanted to leave you with some physical contact to remember me by." He twirled her expertly with a motion that brought her even closer.

"Bill, please. We're the only two people on the floor. Everyone's watching."

"You're the one who's wearing red and winning jackpots. Despite all your fine speeches, you seem determined to call attention to yourself," he teased.

"I certainly do not. I—" She stopped talking abruptly when he kissed her hair. "Don't."

"Can't help it. I like the way you smell."

With immense relief she heard the bandleader encourage other couples to dance, now that the "celebrity" had been honored.

"I really was going to forget about you, you know," Bill said softly into her ear. "Jason and I took in a nightclub act in the café. He met someone there he wanted to spend some time alone with, so I wandered down to the casino, and there you were, causing a ruckus."

"It wasn't my fault."

"If you're so conservative and uninterested in men, why did you buy this red outfit?"

She couldn't explain the impulse that had led her to try on the slinky dress in a color she seldom wore.

He held her away from him and gazed into her face as they swayed together. "I think I know why."

"Think anything you like." Her heart pounded at the look in his eyes.

"It fits you like a glove."

"I usually do buy clothes that fit." She couldn't decide which was more unnerving—being held so tightly against his body or being surveyed with such interest. Thank heaven the song was almost finished.

"You're a puzzle, Lila." He nestled her against him once more. "I've always liked figuring out puzzles."

"You won't have time." Her answer sounded breathless and unconvincing. This close, wearing only thin silk, she felt every ripple of his body as they danced.

"Three nights and four days left. And neither of us is going anywhere," he countered softly. Then he kissed the curve of her neck, and she shuddered. "You know you're kidding yourself, Lila," he whispered against her ear.

"You've got to stop this," she choked out. "We're total strangers. I don't even know your last name."

"Windsor," he offered. "I'm Bill Windsor, and you're . . . ?"

"Lila Kedge."

"And something's going on between us, Lila," Bill continued.

"No," she denied, even though she vibrated with every warm breath that caressed her ear.

"Yes," he contradicted, "but that's the end of the song." He stood back and looked at her, his blue gaze gentled by the seductive friction their bodies had created. "Still leaving?"

"Still leaving." She felt heat course through her cheeks as his gaze flicked over her aroused body. She turned and hurried back to the table. "I have a dreadful headache," she said truthfully to Penny as she fumbled in her purse for some money. "But I still want to treat you. Here."

"You do look feverish," Penny said. "Want me to go back with you?"

"I wouldn't dream of it," Lila said. "All I need is an aspirin and a soft bed."

"What was that?" Bill asked, coming up behind her.

"Nothing," Lila said. "Good night, you two." She almost ran out of the lounge.

Back in the cabin, she found the aspirin and gulped down two tablets with a glass of water. Then she undressed quickly, popped her nightgown over her head and crawled into bed. The sheets and pillow felt cool against her heated skin; the gentle rocking of the ship and the thrumming of the engines far below soothed her. She made her mind a blank and gradually the throbbing in her head lessened.

She never got headaches, she thought, at least she hadn't in the past few years. This headache was Bill's fault. If he hadn't flirted with her, if he hadn't deliberately set up that dance, if he hadn't kissed her on the neck...the throbbing began again and Lila pressed her fingers to her temple.

At this moment Bill was dancing with Penny. Maybe Penny, who was a terrific dancer, would make him forget about his interest in Lila. The thought should have quieted the pounding in Lila's head, but instead it became worse.

She'd left a light on for Penny, and she was debating whether to turn it off for the welcome relief of darkness, when a key clicked in the lock and Penny walked in.

Closing the door behind her, she came over to sit on the other bed. "How're you feeling?"

"Better," Lila said. Unfortunately, it was true. Now that she knew Penny wasn't in Bill's arms, she felt much better. "Why are you back so soon?"

Penny smiled wryly. "As luck would have it, I think he likes you more than me. I got my one dance, which proves he's a gentleman of his word, and then he made some excuse about meeting his son for the midnight buffet. He didn't invite me to join them."

"Penny, I'm sorry."

"Don't be. It's not your fault. I just think it's the pits that he apparently prefers someone who doesn't want him to someone who does."

"I told you, it's the marriage thing. He's afraid you look at him and hear wedding bells."

"And he's right," Penny acknowledged with a chuckle, "but I have to steer him away from that fear, I guess, by pretending I'm not in the market for a husband."

"Good luck with that one."

"He may be a hard nut to crack, at that. During our dance I tried to find out a little about him, you know, where he was from, what he did for a living. He sidestepped every question. I don't even know his last name, but that's easy enough to find out."

"It's Windsor," Lila supplied without thinking.

Penny raised one eyebrow. "Oh? When did he tell you?"

"While we were dancing." Damn her big mouth.

"I see."

"Look, Penny, I'm really trying to discourage the guy. I'd love for you to snag him, but I don't think he's snaggable. As I've said about a million times now, I think we should both avoid him for the rest of the cruise. We could probably get our table assignment changed. In fact, let's do that."

Penny gazed at her friend. "All I have to know is, are you interested?"

"No." Lila's headache returned.

"Good." Penny sighed in relief. "Then leave the rest to me." She tapped on her chin with one finger. "Okay. We're scheduled for that horseback ride after we dock in Ensenada tomorrow. I need to find out if Bill's going." She paused. "Come to think of it, there's a list on the bulletin board by the purser's office. Now that I know Bill's last name I can check the list. Be right back."

After the door closed behind Penny, Lila plopped back against her pillow with a groan. This whole mess reminded her of the days when Penny had tried to charm certain boys in high school. Most of the schemes had failed miserably, and this one had all the signs of doing the same.

But the current situation had a twist that hadn't existed in high school. Penny had never gone after someone who wanted Lila, instead. They'd never been rivals. Well, they wouldn't be now, either, Lila vowed, turning over and punching her pillow.

Penny returned with the news that Bill was on the list. "Hey, I have a big favor to ask, roomie," she said. "Since Bill seems to prefer you, I'd have a clearer field if you didn't join the ride tomorrow."

"No problem," Lila replied. "I won't go. I wasn't too wild about the idea, anyway. Horses scare me a little, as you know. I'll shop in Ensenada instead."

"Thanks, hon." Penny leaned down and gave Lila a hug. "I'm sure glad I brought my tight jeans."

"Penny—"

"Don't say it. You're going to advise me not to be too obvious, right?"

"Right."

"I won't. But I'm wearing those sexy jeans. A man with a physique like Bill's surely appreciates a nice bottom on a woman."

Lila wanted to tell her that it wouldn't matter if she went riding tomorrow looking like Lady Godiva. Bill seemed to be the kind of guy who would reject anything that was shoved into his face. Lila understood that, because she was the same way. But she said nothing.

THE NEXT MORNING Lila discovered she had a choice between eating breakfast in the dining room or eating it buffet style on the promenade deck. She chose the latter and managed to avoid Bill.

She kept to her cabin until after the ship docked in Ensenada and the contingent of horseback riders had left for town. When enough time had elapsed for them to be long gone into the hills surrounding the small Mexican village, Lila dressed in a bright flowered sundress and headed down the gangplank.

Strolling toward town, she enjoyed feeling firm ground under her feet again. A taxi stopped and the driver offered her a ride, but she decided to walk the short distance. She was used to more physical exercise than she'd had in the past two days. Perhaps that explained her headache the night before, she thought.

The autumn sky was cloudless, the sun warm overhead as Lila passed the outskirts of town and entered the main street lined with open-air shops. The atmosphere was familiar; she'd visited the border town of

Tijuana often and was used to the colorful display of
serapes and sombreros, polished wood carvings and
crepe-paper piñatas. Yet Ensenada was a different town,
and she anticipated with pleasure the prospect of looking for new treasures and bargaining with the shopkeepers. She'd pick up something for each of her
daughters, and maybe a toy for the baby, too.

She wasn't the only person from the cruise wander-
ing through town, she noticed. As the ship's passengers walked the streets, the shopkeepers coaxed them
to come in and buy. Most of the passengers did just that,
Lila noticed with satisfaction. She imagined that the
town's economy depended almost entirely on visits
from cruise ships.

Inside the cool interior of a shop filled with the pun-
gent scent of leather goods, Lila paused to consider
handbags for Tracey and Sarah. Soon, she was dickering with the clerk about the price, but her bargaining
was interrupted when a man entered her peripheral vision. *It couldn't be*, she thought. But it was. Her
thumping heart confirmed it. Bill stopped, not ten feet
from her, and fingered a serape. For some reason he
hadn't taken the horseback ride.

Lila's relaxed enjoyment of the day disappeared and
she backed farther into the shop. At that moment Bill
looked directly at her and smiled, and she knew with
absolute certainty that this meeting was no accident.
He'd known where she was all along, and he'd followed her into town. Putting aside the handbags and
telling the clerk she'd be right back, Lila squared her
shoulders and walked toward the front of the shop.
She'd put an end to this, once and for all.

3

"YOU FOLLOWED ME," Lila accused, steeling herself against the effect of Bill's welcoming smile, so dazzlingly white against his sun-bronzed skin. "You canceled the horseback ride and followed me here."

"Yep." He slid his hands into his pockets and assumed the stance of a man determined to hold his position.

So damned cocky, she thought, *standing there in his aviator sunglasses and shirtsleeves rolled back, as if he knew my weakness for strong arms that can—*she reined in her imagination. "You're wasting your time." Her statement didn't ring out with as much force as she would have liked. Despite her resolve to the contrary, she was reacting to him.

"I don't think so."

Self-confidence was sexy, and she'd bet he knew it. "You are pretty darned sure of yourself, mister."

"Lila, I haven't lived forty-seven years and learned nothing about a woman's reaction to me. If you really didn't like me at all, I'd know it and I'd have taken that horseback ride. Hell, I might even have reconsidered your friend Penny."

Lila turned away. "I wish you wouldn't say things like that. I already feel guilty about Penny. She's so good-hearted, and I'd never do anything to hurt her."

"Is that what this is all about? Not hurting your friend?"

Lila shook her head. "No, it's more than that. I meant what I said on the ship last night." She glanced up at him. "I have plenty on my plate without adding someone like you." *Someone who makes me think of private rooms, and soft beds, and skin touching skin.*

He laughed. "*Someone like me?* Keep giving me this kind of pep talk and I'll begin to think you prefer the guys who put too much importance on their laundry."

She considered his statement. Was it actually easier to deal with selfish, boring men who'd never really excite her or inflict more than superficial wounds to her heart?

"Aha. Gotcha," he said softly. "Come on, have a margarita with me in the cantina. We'll talk."

"I . . . I have shopping to do." The warm sun and the festival atmosphere of the town were wearing her down, not to mention the enticing scent of his aftershave and the seductive allure of his smile. Avoiding him for Penny's sake now seemed like a schoolgirl's problem that could be easily handled and resolved by two adults. Then too, he'd issued a challenge by insinuating that she couldn't deal with a vibrant, sophisticated man.

"I'll help you shop," he said. "Was there something in here you wanted?"

"Purses, one for each of my daughters," she said, allowing him to guide her back through the narrow aisles. The clerk approached, his eyes alight at the prospect of a sale.

"Your daughters?" Bill asked. "How old are they? High school age?"

"Bill, you don't have to flatter me. Tracey is twenty-four and Sarah is twenty. And while we're on the subject, I'm forty-five." She nodded to the clerk and pointed to a purse hanging by its strap. "I'd like to look at that one again, please."

"You're that ancient, huh?" Bill surveyed her with a grin. "You carry your years well."

"You're making fun of me." She examined the stitching on the purse.

"Very gently. You think that recitation of ages will scare me off? I agree with Coco Chanel. A woman's not interesting until she's over forty."

"That sounds like a line, Bill."

"But it isn't, Lila."

"Oh, I forgot. You don't need lines to get women, do you? They just automatically fall at your feet."

Bill turned to the clerk. "You see how she picks on me? All I want to do is buy the lady a drink, and that's how she treats me. Don't you think she should be nicer?"

The clerk glanced from one to the other, hesitating.

"Never mind," Lila said to the confused clerk. "Here's my bottom price for the purse, because I'm buying two of them."

The clerk sighed and suggested a higher amount. Lila shook her head. He came down another few pesos, and she shook her head and started to leave.

"Where are you going?" Bill demanded, following her. "Don't you want those for your daughters?"

"I'll get them," she said in a low voice. "Don't worry."

"Lord spare us, you're a bargain hunter," Bill said, as the clerk came after them with a lower offer.

"That's right," Lila confirmed. "And I'll bet you can't abide bargain hunters, so we can part company right now and save ourselves lots of trouble."

"Nice try. Only a fool would expect a woman to agree with him on everything. Listen, I'll be right outside, and when you've finished your transaction, we'll have our margarita. I understand there's no dickering over drink prices at the cantina, so I'll handle that part."

"Bill, this isn't going to work. We're not getting along," Lila protested as the clerk begged her to take his lowest offer, still higher than her bottom price.

"Sure we are. Now do your thing." Bill leaned down and dropped a quick kiss on her cheek before walking out of the shop.

His kiss distracted her so much that she agreed to the clerk's next offer, despite her former decision to pay nothing more than her last bid.

The clerk's leathery face crinkled in amusement as he glanced from her flushed cheeks to the man waiting outside in the sunlight. "Just like on 'Love Boat,' *señora*," he said with a chuckle. "You and the *señor* will end up together."

"I don't think so," Lila said. "We're real people, not some characters from a TV show. Life's more complicated than that."

"Not always, *señora*," said the clerk, wrapping the purses in vanilla-colored paper and tying the parcel with string. "Anything else?"

"I forgot the baby," Lila muttered, remembering she'd decided to pick out something for Stevie.

"Pardon?"

"That little chair." Lila pointed to a brightly painted wooden chair with a woven straw seat. "He'll love having a piece of furniture his size. How much?"

The clerk named a price.

"Fine. I'll take it."

"Fine?" He looked at her in disbelief.

Belatedly she realized she hadn't tried to bring him down on the price. "Well, it's not enough to quibble over, is it?" she said with a sheepish grin.

"Not when one is in a hurry, *señora*." The clerk winked and handed her the chair.

"But I'm..." Lila decided not to finish her denial. She already looked foolish enough. "Thank you," she said, taking the wrapped parcel and the chair.

"*Gracias, señora*," the clerk said, smiling broadly. "Have a good time."

She forced herself to walk at a casual pace as she approached Bill. He was whistling softly in tune with a band of mariachis playing "El Rancho Grande" in front of the cantina down the street.

"All set," she said.

He glanced at her in surprise. "Already? I thought the negotiations would take a heck of a lot longer than that."

"Well, they didn't."

He eyed the chair. "How old did you say you daughters are?"

"I have a ten-month-old grandson," she said, gauging his reaction. "I'm a grandmother, Bill."

He clutched his chest and staggered backward. "A grandmother! Anything but that! Say it isn't true."

"Good grief," Lila muttered. "I'd better get you to that cantina before you make a complete spectacle of yourself."

"Let me carry the chair, Granny," Bill said with a grin as he took it from her. "Wouldn't want someone of your advanced age to tax herself. Did you get a good price on this stuff?" he added as they started down the street.

"Pretty good. I've done better in Tijuana, but I'm used to the shops there."

"I hardly ever get down to Mexico."

"Oh?" Lila asked. "Where do you live?" When he smiled instead of answering, she knew she'd blown her cover of indifference. "I was simply making polite conversation," she added defensively.

"Uh-huh."

"Really I don't care to know where you live."

"Of course you don't. I live in Mission Viejo. Your turn."

"This is pointless."

"But so polite. Where do you call home, Lila of the beautiful brown eyes?"

"Not that it makes any difference, but I live in La Jolla."

"A mere eighty miles south of Mission Viejo," he pointed out.

"A long eighty miles south."

"Maybe a few margaritas will shorten the distance. This way," he said, guiding her through the open doors of the cantina. Ceiling fans spun overhead and ferns cascaded from baskets and clay pots. "Over there," he said, easing her toward a corner table. "I'll take your package."

She handed him her bundle and glanced around. The cantina overflowed with cruise passengers hoisting frosty glasses while brown-skinned waiters and waitresses brought orders of food fragrant with the aroma of chili peppers. Everyone in the room seemed ready to soak up the moment and leave their cares behind, in the traditional Mexican way, for mañana.

Bill held her chair and she smiled up at him. "This is lovely. Thanks for asking me."

"You're welcome. I'm working hard to overcome this image you have that all men are fixated on laundry." He sat down and laid his sunglasses on the straw place mat in front of him. "How am I doing?" he asked, gazing at her.

She hadn't fully realized the power those blue eyes possessed. The night before, subdued light had muted their effect, but today Bill's gaze sparkled intensely. She swallowed. "Not bad," she said.

His lazy smile indicated he'd understood all she hadn't said. He glanced up as the waitress approached. "Two gigantic margaritas, please."

The waitress nodded and left, returning moments later with salt-rimmed goblets the size of soup bowls.

"That should do it," Bill said and lifted his glass toward Lila. "Here's to smooth sailing."

She touched the rim of her glass to his and sparkles of salt littered the table. "To smooth sailing," she echoed, and tasted her drink. "Mmm." The first sip cooled her dry throat. The second loosened all the little muscles in her body she'd had no idea she was clenching.

"I knew this was a good idea." Bill leaned back in his chair and regarded her with satisfaction. "You look terrific when you're relaxed. You're not so bad tense, either, but I like this better."

"I probably should be tense. I have no idea what I'll tell Penny."

"Do you have to tell her anything? I thought that sort of stuff disappeared after high school."

"I know what you mean, and it must seem silly to you," Lila said, as loyalty and honesty warred in her head. "But you see, she asked me not to go on the horseback ride so I wouldn't present any competition. Now here I am having a drink with you, which doesn't seem like a friend's normal course of action. I don't want her to think I'm sabotaging her."

"You're not." He nursed his drink. "I am."

"Maybe." She watched the movement of his throat as he swallowed the cool green liquid. The crisp blue and white of his open-necked shirt emphasized the depth of his tan, and she wondered if all of his body was the same golden hue. She imagined sun-bleached hair, the same shade as on his forearms, swirling over the muscled expanse of his chest. She sighed.

"Anything wrong?"

"Uh, no," she said, thinking quickly. "I suppose I still feel guilty, that's all. You yourself said if I'd showed absolutely no interest, you might have reconsidered Penny."

"Scratch that." He put down his glass and leaned his arms on the table while he gazed at her. "Penny doesn't hold a candle to you. She may be a wonderful woman, but nothing happens to me when I look at her. Now, when I look at you, all kinds of exciting things happen to me. That's not her fault or yours. It just is. And that kind of thing doesn't happen to me all that often, either, Lila."

His voice slid over her, bringing a languorous warmth that threatened to destroy all her reservations, including her concern about Penny's feelings. She felt a little foolish about voicing that problem, anyway. "All right, never mind about Penny. The fact is, I came on this cruise to relax, not to find someone with whom to have a relationship."

A hint of a smile curved his mouth and he slid one finger down the length of her arm where it lay on the table. "They might go together."

She moved her arm. It tingled so much she fought the urge to rub the part he'd touched. "I doubt it."

He picked up his glass. "Depends on whether you look on a relationship as a problem or a solution." He took a drink and flicked a grain of salt from his lower lip with his tongue.

Transfixed, she stared at his mouth. Such smooth lips. If only, for just a moment, she could...but no. She was creating a fantasy loaded with potential problems. Overhead the ceiling fans whispered, while around them people told jokes and laughed with the lightness of those enjoying the present. Perhaps they could afford that luxury, but she had responsibilities, problems to face when she returned to L.A. She realized Bill was watching her and that her heated gaze had probably told him volumes.

"Talk to me, Lila," he urged gently.

What she was imagining had little to do with talk, but she decided that she'd better make some safe conversation, and fast. She took another sip of her margarita and cleared her throat. "So, what do you do for a living?" she asked, refashioning her expression to one of polite interest.

He chuckled. "Okay, Lila. We can do this routine, if you like. I'm an auto mechanic."

Her mouth dropped open. She'd imagined he was a stockbroker, corporation head, perhaps even a restaurant owner.

"Disappointed?" he asked.

"Well, no, not really," she fumbled. "But you don't look like my picture of a mechanic."

"I left my oil-stained coveralls at home," he said with a faint smile. "Jason didn't think they'd be appropriate on a cruise. Maybe I still have some axle grease under my fingernails, though, if you need convincing." He put his hand on the table close to hers.

"I believe you." She didn't take the thinly disguised invitation to touch his hand. "I was surprised, that's all."

In one easy movement he covered the short distance necessary to make contact and cradled her hand in his. "Then I'll look at your fingernails and see if I can guess what you do," he said.

"They won't tell you," she said, as alarm bells in her head went off in response to his touch.

"No?" He looked at her hand and studied the careful manicure, the rich red polish. Then he turned it palm up and stroked his thumb across the base of her fingers. "Beautiful nails, no calluses. You're in business. Office work."

Lila shivered. "True."

"And because you're so reluctant to allow anything new into your life, I'll bet you have lots of responsibility in that office. You're in charge, and conscious of what that kind of responsibility entails."

"True again." Oh, how she wished that she didn't crave the warmth of his caress, that she didn't imagine him stroking her—all over. She closed her eyes for a moment.

He brought her palm to his lips and placed a lingering kiss there. "I'm sorry your cares weigh so heavily on you," he said.

She gazed at him, her heart thumping. "So am I."

"Real estate's a tough game."

She snapped to attention. "How did you know I was in real estate?"

His hand enveloped hers, holding her prisoner. "I could tell you I'm a mind reader, and right now I wish that were true. But I didn't guess. I asked Penny last night. She was a little upset with me because I wanted to talk about you."

Penny. Lila's conscience assailed her again. How could she face Penny if she allowed this attraction to blossom, knowing how much Penny longed to find a second husband, and especially after vowing that the last thing in the world she herself wanted was a man in her life? She pulled her hand away from his. "I—thank you for the drink, but I'd better go back to the ship," Lila said. "I really hadn't meant to stay in town so long."

Bill sighed. "Fool that I am, I reminded you of Penny again, right?"

"Well, yes, but you also reminded me that I really don't want to get involved right now." She pushed back her chair and stood. "Thanks again for the drink, and the . . . conversation."

"We'll go together," he said, also standing. "I'll get us a taxi."

"I'd better go alone."

"At least let me carry your packages," he said, reaching for the small chair and the bundle containing the purses.

"Bill." She put her hand on his arm and quickly took it away again as the impulse to caress him nearly overwhelmed her. "The timing on this is no good. I'm here as Penny's companion while she's looking for a special someone. Starting up with you would be inappropriate and hurtful to my best friend, not to mention unwise for me." She glanced away from him but he took her chin between his thumb and forefinger and brought her gaze back to his. She read barely checked desire and frustration in his eyes.

"Then this is goodbye?" he said softly.

"Yes, in a manner of speaking." She trembled at being so temptingly near him.

"Then you won't begrudge me this," he said, and kissed her.

She was so startled that she didn't resist. He was good at it, but she'd known he would be. His lips coaxed the beginning of a response from her, and then abruptly he lifted his head. "Goodbye, Lila Kedge," he whispered, smiling gently.

Her dazed reverie gave way to anger. He didn't take her declaration seriously. He expected that one expertly delivered, not quite consummated kiss would bring her right into his arms. She'd show him she was made of stronger stuff than that! "Goodbye, Bill Windsor," she said, her voice shaking only a little. She picked up her packages, turned on her heel, and left the cantina.

Behind her, Bill stared at the doorway long after she'd disappeared.

The waitress approached and tentatively touched his sleeve. "Another margarita, *señor?*"

Bill grimaced before glancing down at the waitress. "What I want," he said, "is a double Scotch on the rocks."

"BILL DIDN'T TAKE the horseback ride after all," Penny said, barging into the cabin. She smelled of dust and animal sweat. "But maybe that was just as well, because I found out tons of information about him from Jason, his son. Wait'll you hear this."

"Penny, there's something I—"

"Look at you, curled up with a book!" Penny threw her blouse on the floor and inched out of her tight jeans. "I'll bet you've been hiding away in this cabin all day, haven't you?"

"I went shopping, and—"

"Oh? What did you get?" *Kissed*, Lila thought. "Purses for Tracey and Sarah, and that little chair for Stevie." She pointed to the corner of the cabin where she'd stored the chair. "And by the way, speaking of Bill—"

"Let me tell you, he's a better catch than I even imagined, Lila. Jason insisted on this cruise specifically to matchmake for his father, and he's willing to help me bait the trap. I've got the son on my side, and that's a big step in the right direction, wouldn't you say?"

"I...I guess so." Lila's courage failed her. She'd wanted to tell Penny everything that had happened today, but now.... How could she predict the outcome of a combined campaign waged by Jason and Penny? Maybe Bill wouldn't be able to resist. After all, Penny was a sexy, terrific woman and Bill wasn't exactly made of stone. She could certainly attest to that.

"Mind if I use the shower before you?" Penny stripped and headed for the small bathroom.

"Nope."

"I'll leave the door open so I can tell you about Bill. Can you believe he's a car mechanic?" Penny called over the sound of the spray.

"No kidding." Lila closed her eyes. She'd get rid of this inconvenient attraction to Bill. Her best friend wanted him, and deserved him, too, for that matter.

"Well, he repairs Jaguars," Penny continued, "so it's a lot more glamourous than it sounds at first, and he makes good money, according to Jason. But get this— Jason thinks his dad is lonely."

Lila thought of the way Bill had kissed her today and almost laughed out loud. A man who could kiss like that was no more lonely than he chose to be. "Why does Jason think that?" she asked. "I got the impression Bill could have as many dates as he could fit into his calendar."

"Yeah, but he doesn't allow himself to fall for any of the women he dates. Instead, he puts all his energy into racing cars, and Jason says he's getting more reckless." Penny turned off the shower.

"What exactly are you saying, Pen?"

"Jason thinks his dad needs a wife to settle him down." Penny walked into the room with a towel wrapped around her while she dried her wet hair with a second one. "Someone who needs him, someone to drain off that excess energy, someone who'd give him a reason not to end up in a mess of twisted metal." Penny flipped her damp hair back from her face and looked at Lila. "I'm going to be that someone."

4

"OH, PENNY, don't tell me you're going to save him from himself," Lila protested with a groan.

"What's wrong with that? Jason thinks—"

"Jason's a kid, with a lot to learn. Now that his mother's not around he's probably taken too much responsibility for his dad's welfare."

"I agree, and that's where I come in. Jason's leaving for the East Coast right after this trip, and he'd love to know a caring woman was keeping an eye on his father."

"Did it ever occur to you that Bill enjoys taking chances with his racing? That he prefers dating several women instead of being committed to one? That he's perfectly content with his life the way it is?"

Penny gazed at her. "Jason says he's not, and I'd expect a man's own flesh and blood to know. Lila, you've been against me on this all along. Are you quite sure you don't want Bill for yourself? Five years is a long time to be single, and I wouldn't blame you for thinking in terms of marriage, especially with a hunk like Bill around."

"Marriage? Get real, Penny. Most guys demand more out of marriage than I'm willing to give." That much was true, she thought. But as for wanting Bill, she'd plead guilty to that, if Penny asked the right question.

Fortunately for both of them, Penny had only focused on the marriage angle.

"Okay, then the field's still clear for me. Jason wants a stepmother, and I want a husband. Jason's going to have a talk with his dad before dinner, put in a good word for me. How about this green dress for tonight?" Penny pulled a slinky floor-length gown from the closet.

"You look wonderful in that." Lila had to admit that she didn't know Bill well enough to predict how he'd respond to Jason and Penny's assault. Maybe his frustration with Lila this afternoon would send him straight into Penny's arms. Lila had no business interfering with that. If she had no long-term goal concerning Bill, the noble thing would be to step back and let Penny have her shot. Which she would do. "I'm really not in the mood for a big dinner tonight," she said. "I think I'll have something sent to the cabin, instead."

"No dinner?" Penny sat on the bed and scrutinized Lila. "Are you sick?"

"To tell the truth, I had a huge margarita when I was in town today, and I'm still feeling the effects of it."

"My goodness." Penny shook her head. "You're just not a party girl, are you?"

"Come on, Penny, you know I'm not. That's one reason we get along so well. That's why you brought me, isn't it?"

Penny looked taken aback. "Of course not. I asked you because you're my best friend."

"I know. And you're mine. I love you dearly. But you expect me to be a bit of a wet blanket, don't you? A kind of comforting anchor, so you won't stray too far in the storm? Be honest, Penny. If I suddenly became wild and crazy, you'd flip out."

"I . . . I don't know. I'll have to think about that. Anyway, coming to dinner wouldn't exactly be wild and crazy."

That's what you think, Lila mused. "I suppose not," she said aloud, "but I'm not really in the mood to get dolled up and plow my way through six courses."

"We both missed out on dinner last night because of the storm, and now you're not going tonight, either. You'd better promise to eat the last dinner tomorrow night, at least."

Lila smiled. By tomorrow night something would be resolved one way or the other. "Okay, I promise."

"Great. My goodness, it's late. I'd better slither into this dress and put on my war paint. Tonight could be the first night of the rest of my life."

"I hope it is, Penny," Lila said truthfully.

TWO HOURS LATER Penny stormed back into the room. "That man can jolly well wind his racing car around a telephone pole, for all I care."

"Troubles?" Lila put down the book she'd been unsuccessfully trying to read.

"You were right, Lila. I'll have to ignore the packaging on this one, because it turns out he's all wrapped up in himself."

"What about his talk with Jason? Didn't that help?"

"If anything, Jason made things worse. After dinner Bill took us both aside and told us in no uncertain terms to mind our own business. He said he had no intention of ever marrying again, and if he ever did anything that crazy, he wouldn't pick a woman who'd discourage him from taking risks."

Lila felt a glow of pride. *Way to go, Bill.* "I'm sorry, Penny."

"Aren't you going to say I told you so?"

Lila shook her head.

"You can if you want. I should have listened to you. Usually when I do, everything turns out okay." Penny sat on the bed next to Lila. "And I've thought about what you said. You're right about that, too. I count on your steadiness. If you'd suddenly gone cavorting off with Bill, for example, I would have been thrown off balance."

Lila gazed into her friend's eyes. "That's exactly what he wanted me to do."

Penny hesitated. "You mean last night, when you were dancing?"

"Well, yes, but today, too. He followed me into town and we . . . had a drink together."

Penny's expression tightened. "Why didn't you tell me?"

"Because I thought maybe you'd work something out with him through Jason. After all, I rejected him today, and for all I knew he'd—"

"Take me as leftovers?" Penny stood up and paced the room. "Thanks. Thanks a lot."

"Pen, I was only trying—"

"Look, it's bad enough that he's not the least bit interested in me, even after I wore my sexiest dress and turned on all the charm." Penny's lower lip trembled and her eyes filled. "But now I find out that he's been trying to seduce my best friend and she didn't even tell me!"

"Penny, please."

"Worst of all, I can't even blame you. But excuse me if I don't feel like hanging around tonight and being pals. The newlyweds are going into town and they've asked me to join them. I came back to see if you wanted to go, but if you don't mind . . ."

"I'll stay here."

"Maybe you should go look for Bill. I'm sure he'd be excited about that."

"Penny, for heaven's sake!"

"Why not? You're a perfect match. Neither of you has the guts to chance a real relationship, a real commitment. All either of you can talk about is your blessed independence. You deserve each other!"

"I'm going for a walk on deck." Lila shoved her feet into a pair of canvas shoes and grabbed a sweater. She'd always hated confrontations, and Penny seemed determined to prolong this one. Why had she agreed to this stupid cruise? Penny had convinced her it would be a chance to get away from the pressure at home. Ha! The pressure on this ship outclassed her problems with the agency and her daughters by a long shot.

"Fine," Penny called after her. "I'll be gone when you get back."

Lila took several brisk turns around the deck. She probably looked silly doing it, she thought, considering the relaxed mood of everyone she passed. The ship was strung with lights from bow to stern and the sound of laughter and tinkling glasses traveled over the harbor towards the sparkling lights of Ensenada. She was out of sync with all of it and longed for Dorothy's red shoes, so she could click her heels together and magically find herself at home.

Fortunately, Penny's anger wouldn't last long. She was hurt now and lashing out at Lila, the most convenient target. Good old Lila, steady as a rock, a port in a storm. Lila shoved her hands into her pockets and walked faster. Who would have guessed that a man would prefer her to Penny? It had never happened before, but then, Lila hadn't put herself in many situations like this with Penny, at least, not since high school.

Gradually, guiltily, Lila acknowledged the secret elation she felt at being chosen over Penny, who with her blond good looks had always been the flashier of the two friends. People had often told Lila she was a late bloomer. Maybe the tag was beginning to crystallize.

Not that it mattered. She needed male admirers like a hole in the head. Still, it was nice to know that she'd been judged desirable by a man with Bill's experience. Maybe she'd attracted mostly nerds—his word—because that was all she'd expected to attract.

Lila felt much better by the time she returned to the cabin. She dressed for bed and curled into her bunk with the book that now seemed far more interesting than it had a few hours ago. Tomorrow they'd leave Ensenada, and by the following morning she'd be home having learned two things—that she was more attractive than she'd thought, and that she'd never again venture on one of Penny's trips.

Of course, Penny wasn't likely to ask her, Lila thought ruefully. Her recent outburst aside, Penny wanted to protect the friendship as much as Lila did. They'd been through too much, weathered too many years together to give up on each other now. Lila found her place in the novel and began to read.

A knock at the door startled her out of a torrid love scene. She had no trouble imagining who it was. She just wouldn't answer.

The knock came again, louder this time. "I'll bet you're in there, Lila," Bill called through the door. "Playing possum."

She snuggled farther down under the covers. The door was locked; the window shade was drawn. He'd have no way of knowing she was there if she kept quiet. Then her nose began to itch.

"Lila, this is ridiculous. You missed dinner, just to avoid me, and now you're hiding in your cabin. I'm not going to bite. Can't we talk like two civilized people?"

This attraction isn't civilized, she thought, pressing her finger to the base of her nose. The sneeze she was suppressing was the most persistent she could remember. Damn. She didn't want to deal with him, now or ever.

"Lila, come on. I know you're in there. Penny told me you were staying in your cabin tonight."

Well, thanks, Penny, she thought. *Now we're even*. She'd just about subdued the sneeze when the phone rang. With Bill outside her door, the phone call had to be from Penny on shore or from one of Lila's kids, and she couldn't ignore any of those people. She picked up the receiver and murmured a soft greeting.

"Lila? It's Penny. I'm at the cantina and I've been thinking. I'm sorry about what I said."

"It's okay," Lila whispered.

"Why are you whispering? Are you sick?"

Lila groaned. It was no use. "No, Penny, I'm fine. I must have had something in my throat. And I'm sorry, too, about the way things turned out."

"You're my best friend, Lila. I never want anything to come between us." Penny sounded as if she'd just had the same size margarita Lila had drunk that afternoon.

"Nothing will, Penny. I'll see you soon. And thanks for calling."

"I just couldn't let any more minutes go by without apologizing," Penny said. "We're having a great time here. Want to come on in and join us?"

"Uh, no, no. I'll just stay here with my interesting book."

"All right. Tomorrow we'll have a good day, just you and me, okay?"

"Okay. 'Bye."

"Goodbye, my dear friend."

Lila hung up the phone and waited for the response from the other side of the door.

"Well, Lila," Bill said, "now I know for sure you're in there, and you're deliberately avoiding me. Wouldn't you call that a little childish?"

"No." She hated the petulant tone that seemed to prove him right.

"Okay. I know when I'm beaten. But in case you change your mind once we're on shore, I'm writing down my address and telephone number in Mission Viejo. I'll slip it under the door."

She hugged her book to her chest. "Whatever. I won't call."

"You never know. Things might change. Anyway, I won't bother you for the rest of the cruise. So long, Lila."

After the sound of his footsteps had died away, she waited a few more seconds and walked to the door. No note. She dropped to her knees and peered through the crack but couldn't see a piece of paper. The idiot must have done a poor job of sliding it under the door. She couldn't let Penny come and find it.

As she opened the door, she sensed a motion beside her and whirled around. "Bill, you maniac! Where the devil did you come from?"

He took one hand from behind his back. He was holding his shoes. "I snuck. Or is it sneaked?"

"I think the verb is snaked." She backed through the door. "Good night, Mr. Windsor."

He braced his hand against it, holding it open. "Just a minute. That was a very clever bit I just engineered. Don't I even deserve a few words in exchange?"

"You just got them. Good night." She tried to push his hand away from the door, but with little effect.

"Lila, it isn't either of our faults that Penny's disappointed. It's Penny's problem."

"Perhaps, but I'm not planning to add to that problem."

"So you'll sacrifice whatever fun we could have?"

"That's right. Now move your hand so I can close the door."

"Look, I understand that you wanted to give Penny a shot, but we wouldn't be taking anything away from her. If you won't give me a chance, you'll be taking away a lot we could have together."

Lila noticed that a couple approaching them along the corridor was watching the scene with great interest. She didn't relish this kind of conversation overheard. "Get in here," she muttered, opening the door.

"That's more like it." Bill closed the door behind him.

"Don't jump to conclusions." She put her hands on her hips. "I just don't want the whole world to hear what I have to say. I'm not going to have an affair with you, Bill Windsor. It would strain my relationship with my best friend, and you're not worth it."

He grinned and stepped toward her. "I can't let a remark like that go unchallenged."

"Haven't you heard anything I've said?" She retreated a step.

"You bet. The spoken and unspoken."

Lila groaned. "I never should have had that drink with you today. I knew this would happen. Now you think—"

"That's right."

"Bill, please go. Penny could arrive any minute."

"We could leave together. My cabin's not far from here."

"What do you expect me to do? Leave a note for Penny telling her I'm in your cabin?"

He shrugged. "Sounds logical to me."

"No." She turned away from him and wrapped her arms protectively around herself. "Despite the signals you may have picked up, I'm not the sort of woman who throws herself into a man's arms when I hardly know him. Especially if there's a chance that doing that will hurt a woman I've cared about for thirty years."

"If the situation were reversed, don't you think that Penny would be in my cabin tonight without a second thought about you?"

"That's different. Penny's in the market. I'm not. When I agreed to take this cruise with her, I expected to spend time alone if she found the right guy." She felt his hands on her shoulders and quivered. "Don't."

"You're a good friend, but I'll bet that Penny's a good friend, too. She wouldn't ask you to sacrifice your own pleasure for her sake." He turned her gently to face him. "Answer me this. Suppose Penny had nothing to do with you and me. What then?"

Lila trembled. Without the threat of Penny returning from Ensenada, would she resist the lure of those seductive blue eyes? The longer she looked into them, the more she quickened with desire.

"I thought as much. Hey, relax, pretty woman."

She allowed him to knead her tight shoulder muscles until her arms hung limp at her sides. He had such knowing fingers. She could easily imagine how he might—no, she wouldn't think about that. But as he touched her, she could think of little else.

"Okay, here's how it is," Bill continued, massaging warmth into her shoulders. "You and I have about thirty-six hours left on this barge together. I'd love to spend most of them kissing every naked inch of you."

She stiffened. "Bill—"

"Easy. This is a suggestion, not an assault. I think you'd get a lot out of the experience, and so would I. I hadn't planned on something like this when I agreed to the cruise, and neither had you, but I think we'd be fools to lose the chance."

"What about Jason? I thought you were supposed to spend some father-son time with him?"

Bill chuckled. "Jason found himself a redhead on the horseback ride. I think that's one reason he plotted with Penny to get me nabbed. He'll be indisposed for the rest of the trip, I imagine, and he didn't want to feel guilty about it."

"So you have some time on your hands?"

"Let's say I don't have to make a difficult choice."

"Nevertheless, I have Penny, and—"

"Dammit." He pulled her roughly into his arms. "Forget Penny and think of this," he muttered, covering her mouth with his.

He held nothing back. The power of his unrestrained needs reverberated through her until she pressed against him to absorb the throbbing beat. Whispering encouragement, he cupped her breast and plunged his tongue into her mouth once more. She couldn't remember a whirlpool of sensation like this—ever. She moaned as her body warmed for him, moistened for him, undulated for him.

"If this isn't a hell of a note!"

They both whirled toward the open cabin door where Penny stood, gray eyes narrowed in anger. "Tell me, was this jerk here when I called a while ago?"

"No, I mean, sort of," Lila stammered, searching her spinning memory for the truth. "Penny, it's not what you think."

"Correction," Bill said, "it's something like what you think. I've been after Lila ever since last night, but she won't have me."

Penny's laugh was bitter. "That isn't the way I'd call it."

"Call it any way you want," Bill said, anger rising in his voice, too. "But you have one loyal friend here, who won't allow herself a few hours of pleasure because it might hurt your feelings. I was just trying to convince her that you wouldn't be that selfish, but I could be wrong."

"Bill, just leave," Lila said, adjusting her nightgown. "You've said quite enough."

"Don't bother, Billy-boy. I'm going to the bar." Penny started walking away. "You two carry on. I'd advise putting a Do Not Disturb sign on the door, though. That way I can tell when I can come back and go to bed without interrupting you."

Lila hurried forward. "Penny—"

"Save it, Lila." Penny's eyes glistened with tears. "I get the picture."

After she closed the door, Lila turned on Bill. "See? See what you've done? She's in tears."

"All right, maybe that wasn't the best way for her to get the news, but sooner or later she should figure out that you have your own life, too. You deserve her support as much as she deserves yours. Friendship isn't a one-way street."

"You haven't the foggiest idea what you're talking about. Throughout my divorce, nobody stood by me the way Penny did. She was there for me the whole time, the *whole time.* Now, I'd appreciate it if you'd leave. I'm getting dressed and going up to the bar to try to salvage a valuable relationship."

"Lila, I wish you'd—"

She flung open the door. "Goodbye, Mr. Windsor. Can we not discuss this again, please?"

"Oh, we won't discuss it anymore. The discussion's closed. But if you want to go beyond talk, you know where to find me." He left the cabin without a backward glance.

5

AS SHE SET OUT in search of Penny, Lila remembered that there were several places on the ship that served drinks. She covered them all, ending with the bar in the casino. Penny wasn't there, either. Lila finally found her seated on a stool in front of a dollar slot feeding in tokens with a vengeance.

"Penny, we need to talk."

She didn't look up from the machine. "Is he with you?"

"No. I sent him away. You've got to believe I didn't mean for something like that to happen."

"Why did you let him into our room?" Penny yanked the lever on the machine but with no results. "Typical lousy luck," she mumbled and pushed five more dollar tokens into the slot.

"I let him in because I felt self-conscious discussing private business in the hall in my nightgown. Things sort of . . . got out of hand."

"Looked to me as if everything was *in* hand, everything of yours in his hands, that is." Penny's machine repaid her five tokens and she returned them to the slot. "I still can't believe it. My best friend making out in our room with the guy I wanted."

Lila grabbed Penny's wrist and jerked her off the stool. "Will you stop playing that blasted thing and listen to me?"

Penny stared at her.

"I've tried really hard to discourage him, Penny, and you give me no credit. I'm sorry you found us kissing, but as you should know, he's an exciting, attractive man, and I'm not made of stone! You're not the only one who can be turned on by a good-looking guy."

"Why, get you," Penny whispered, awed. "You're shaking."

"I'm . . . I'm not, either," Lila said, releasing Penny's wrist.

"You are. Come on and sit down." Penny guided her to a small table in the bar. "Have something to drink."

"No, that isn't what I need." Lila held her head in both hands. "I just need you to understand about Bill."

"I'm beginning to. Lila, you've never in your life stood up to me like that. You're changing."

Lila gazed at her friend. "Maybe you're right."

"I'll bet it has to do with that business about not expecting you to rock the boat."

"No pun intended?" Lila smiled faintly.

Penny smiled back. Then she took a deep breath. "We've been pals a long time, and in all those years you've been so dependable. If someone had told me I'd come back to our room and find what I found there...." Penny shrugged. "But I guess people are entitled to change, huh?"

A waitress approached the table and Lila waved her away. "I hope people are entitled to change, Penny. I don't want to lose you as a friend, but maybe I need room to be a little wild and crazy, sometimes."

"You picked a heck of a way to start. Let's face it, I'm spoiled rotten. No man's ever picked you over me, no one except Stan, that is."

"And we both agree he was no prize," Lila said with a chuckle.

Penny leaned her chin on her hand and studied Lila. "You are quite a dish, you know. I just haven't been willing to admit it, but since the divorce, you've really blossomed. To be honest, I was worried when you first tried on that red dress in the store. I looked at you in the dressing-room mirror and thought, my Lord, the woman is gorgeous. Why am I taking her along on this cruise?"

Lila laughed. "You did not!"

"I did so. Then I reminded myself what a stick-in-the-mud you were when it came to men, and I relaxed."

"Now I'll bet you're sorry you asked me."

Penny didn't answer.

"See? You are!"

"No, not when I think it through. I might have made more headway with Bill if you hadn't been along, but the first time I'd have introduced him to you, bingo, he would've been gone. I would have lost him to you sooner or later. So it might as well be sooner."

Lila shook her head. "You would have lost him, but not because he'd met me. He's a lone wolf, Penny. I'll bet he'd have disappeared once the ship had docked."

"Maybe. And maybe you'll have better luck."

"No, I won't, because I'm not getting involved with Bill in the first place."

"Pardon me, Lila honey, but I think what I saw back in the cabin was pretty involved."

"Beyond that," Lila said, flushing.

"Not on my account, I hope. Because you're right. You should be free to do something wild and crazy without me coming unglued. If you want to spend the rest of the cruise in Bill's cabin, I don't want you to hesitate. Not that I won't be green with jealousy, picturing what you two are doing, but I'll survive. In fact, it'll probably do me good."

Lila searched Penny's expression and found no malice in it. "Thanks. It means a lot to me, your saying that."

"So what are you hanging around here for? Go knock on his door before he changes his mind or I revert to my usual bitchy self."

Lila smiled. "No, thanks."

"Lila, you will drive me to distraction. What is your problem?"

"Cold feet," Lila admitted. "I may be getting braver, but that doesn't mean I can march down to his cabin, toothbrush in hand."

"Then I'll call him." Penny started to rise.

"You will not!" Lila grabbed Penny's arm and pulled her back into the chair. "I would never forgive you if you meddled in this, Penny Casper. Let it go."

"I don't get it. First, you lobby for your right to go to bed with this guy, and now you say you don't want to. You confuse me, woman."

"Let's just drop it, okay? We only have thirty-six hours of this cruise left," she said, using Bill's phrase and feeling the jolt of it run through her system. "It's silly to start something at this late date, and besides, what if I liked him too much? He's made no promises—not that I'd want any—but still, after the ship docks, we'd be strangers again. What's the point?"

"You don't know that's what would happen. He might be in for the long haul."

"That could be even worse. I don't want a man permanently in my life."

"In that case, sleep with him and forget him, just like you think he'll do with you."

"I don't know if I can do that. Penny, I have two grown daughters and a grandson, for Lord's sake. I'm a respected businesswoman in La Jolla. No." She shook her head. "It really isn't my style. Come on," she said, rising from the table. "Let's go back to the cabin and get some sleep."

"Same old Lila," Penny said, following her out of the bar. "For a while there, I thought a transformation had taken place, but I guess I was wrong."

"Zip your lip, Pen," Lila said, and dropped back a step to link arms with her best friend.

SHE HADN'T SHOWN UP. Bill couldn't remember the last time he'd waited all night for a woman to arrive. After drifting in and out of sleep until dawn, he heard the tugs' muted whistle and felt the ship move away from the dock. Wearily he dressed and wandered out on deck.

Zipping his windbreaker against the chill, he leaned on the railing above the prow and watched the crew wind ropes thick as a man's arm onto a drum. Two tugboats, each with a necklace of licorice-colored tires, nudged the ship into the morning fog, guiding it away from a fleet of local trawlers. Gulls circled the boats and filled the morning with their rusted-metal cries.

A crewman noticed Bill on the deck above him and waved. "Nice morning."

"Yeah," Bill said, not meaning it. He'd had a long night and he didn't like fog. "Need any help down there?"

The crewman laughed. "You're supposed to be on vacation, man. We do the work. You do the playing."

Bill's answering smile was tight. He'd never been a fan of indolence, and this cruise was the epitome of lazy living. He'd much rather wrestle with the ropes, or better yet, check the nets on the fishing boats nearby. Instead, he had a choice of shuffleboard or poker.

He wondered if that was why he'd been so hell-bent on getting Lila into bed. Was he as attracted to her as he was to the challenge? Something strange was motivating him to pull crazy stunts like that charade last night. Well, he *had* made it in the door, and if her pesky friend hadn't shown up, he might have gotten further than that.

Which, as he considered the incident in dawn's early light, was all pretty sophomoric. He should have outgrown those tricks years ago, but she'd really intrigued him with her combination of come-hither and stay away. She'd been an exciting challenge.

If he ever gave up his independence, which he didn't think he ever would, he'd pick someone like Lila. Jason didn't understand that, of course. He imagined a woman like Penny, cut from the same cloth as his mother, would settle his father right down. Bill felt sorry for the kid—Jason missed the stability that Joan had provided for her son . . . and her husband. Bill hesitated to explain to Jason that her death, devastating though it had been, had also liberated him from the chains of caution. If Jason heard that, he'd accuse his father of disloyalty and lack of concern for those who loved him. Bill knew the speech well—Joan had delivered it often and Jason now carried on the tradition.

No, Bill didn't see himself taking a chance on a permanent relationship with a woman again. But a sexy rendezvous now and then sure perked things up, and he was sorry this one hadn't worked out. Lila was probably a sizzler in bed, and she was a fun sparring partner out of it. The affair could have been neatly circumscribed by the beginning and end of the cruise—an added bonus.

Bill sighed and pushed himself away from the railing. Regretting might-have-beens wasn't his style. Tomorrow morning at this time, he'd be headed home and by noon he'd be under the lift working on Henry Shultz's XJ6. In the meantime, he'd have to scare up some activity on this barge to use up the hours until he could be productive again.

"HEY, YOU PROMISED," Penny said, facing Lila in their cabin. "So far this cruise has been a dud, and I won't have you wimping out on the last dinner. If I'm woman enough to sit at the same table with Bill, after he took me on a tour of rejection city, you can sit there with me."

"Couldn't we just—"

"You're chicken, Lila Kedge, and don't think I don't know it. All day, wherever we went, whatever we did, you jumped every time you heard a male voice. Did you think Bill would sneak up on you or something?"

"I just didn't want to be taken by surprise, that's all."

"Why? Because you might swoon right into his arms?"

"Of course not." Lila mustered as much indignation as possible, considering that Penny swerved very close to the truth. "All right, I'll go to the stupid dinner. He might not even be there, anyway."

"He might not at that, after the way he knocked himself out to seduce you and came up empty. The guy's pride is probably in shreds."

"Don't you dare try to make me feel sorry for him."

"I won't. I'm too busy feeling sorry for me. Whatcha gonna wear?"

Lila walked over to the small closet and opened the bifold door. "My navy suit, I guess."

"Barf. This is supposed to be a gala event. I'm wearing that hot-pink number I showed you. But I guess you're too chicken to get dressed up, in case that scary Bill guy is there," Penny taunted.

"If you weren't my best friend, I'd punch you in the mouth."

"If you weren't my best friend, I'd let you wear that ugly navy suit. Come on, Lila, don't you have something else in there?" Penny nudged her way past Lila and searched the closet. "What's this?" she asked, pulling out a black jersey. "Yow, no back! Did you borrow this from Tracey or something?"

"No, I . . . found it at that little shop by the cove."

"I've never seen it on you."

"I bought it right before the cruise, but I'm not wearing it, Penny. It doesn't look like me at all, and I can't imagine why I thought—"

"You're right. It doesn't look like you, but neither did the red silk. The navy blue suit looks like you. Wear that. It's nice and dependable."

"What kind of crack is that?"

Penny widened her eyes. "Crack? Lila, honey, I'm only saying what you keep saying. I think some woman is impersonating you. She buys sexy clothes, attracts gorgeous men, and fights honestly, toe-to-toe, with her best friend. But that person can't be you."

"I make one little speech about breaking out of a rut and you want me to change my whole approach to life."

Penny eyed her. "I think the expression is—are you gonna fish or cut bait?"

"What are you suggesting?"

"The cruise isn't over, Lila, and I doubt if Bill has lined anyone else up to see it through with him."

"You're encouraging me to have a one-night stand?"

"Your label, not mine. I'm telling you to take something for yourself, before you go back to Tracey and little Stevie, and the office, and the worries about Sarah flunking out. I never realized before how little you give yourself until you pointed it out to me."

"I don't remember pointing out anything of the kind, Penny."

"Maybe you didn't say those exact words, but you talked about how restricted you've felt, being the steady one for everyone else, including me. Why not put away the martyr's crown for a few hours? Come to think of it, you'd make me feel a whole lot better if you did. Thanks to all these revelations, I've got a classic case of the guilties."

Lila gazed at her friend. "Is that really how I've come across? As a martyr?"

"Well . . . yeah, you have, although I didn't put it all together before now. Here's the scenario—wife is cheated on by husband and left with family and business in a shambles. Wife carries on, restores order to family and business, wears navy blue suits a lot, refuses to have much fun. What picture do you get from that?"

"We do have fun," Lila protested. "What about our garage saling?"

"*I* have fun. You are deadly serious."

"I—"

"Unfortunately, we can't stand here and debate any longer." Penny glanced at her watch. "Our seating for dinner begins in twenty minutes. Are you wearing this backless dress or aren't you?"

"I'm wearing it."

"Way to go, Lila! Who knows, before dinner's over you might even reconsider about Bill."

"Chances are you're right about his wounded pride. I really don't expect him to be there." Lila no longer knew how she felt about that.

NEITHER BILL NOR HIS SON was at the table for six when Penny and Lila arrived.

"Hello, again," Eddie, the newlywed, boomed as they sat down. "Long time no see."

Lila noted that his confidence had increased in the past two days—the honeymoon must be going well. "I just never found myself ready to eat at the right seating time," she said.

"Well, this is it, the last night," Eddie commented unnecessarily. "Let's hope we don't have another storm at sea."

"I'm sure we won't," Penny said. "Have you seen Bill?"

"Nope. But I can't imagine him and his son missing the last big meal of the cruise. Babs and I skimped on lunch, so we'd have room. I think we'll have baked

Alaska for dessert, you know, with flames?" He gestured in the air with both hands.

"Yes, I know about baked Alaska," Penny replied with an amused glance at Lila.

Babs, who wore a touch of razor burn on one cheek, glanced admiringly at Lila. "That's a fantastic dress," she said.

"Thank you."

"The pink one's nice, too, Penny," Babs said quickly, "but you know black's so . . . powerful and—"

"I know," Penny said. "Sexy. Can you believe Lila almost didn't wear this tonight? She brought it but was ready to leave it in the closet."

"You should wear it a lot," Babs said, gazing across at Lila. "Especially with those earrings. They're really unusual."

"Antique gold," Lila said, fingering one. "Penny and I found them at a garage sale. I guess the owner didn't know how valuable they were, so I got them for a song."

Penny chuckled. "And they're worth a whole opera. Lila had to get the suckers insured, which didn't please her any."

"I just never believed in having such expensive jewelery, but I love the way they look, so—" Lila shrugged "—I'm stuck with paying insurance on them."

"Insurance on what?" Jason asked, catching the tail end of the conversation as he pulled out his chair.

"Lila's earrings," Penny said. "Where's your dad?"

"I imagine he'll be along."

Lila doubted it, and disappointment tasted bitter on her tongue. The wine steward approached their table; Bill was already late, and the chances of his coming grew slimmer by the minute. She spread her napkin over her lap and wondered how she'd get through the meal.

"Hail, hail, the gang's all here."

Lila's head snapped up and she found herself looking directly into blue eyes that were trained right on her. A wave of relief made her sigh audibly, which in turn embarrassed her so much, she blushed.

"Why, Bill, we were afraid you wouldn't make it," Penny said, squeezing Lila's hand under the table.

"Only a fool would stay away from a banquet like this," Bill said, his gaze moving over all the women but lingering on Lila. "Everyone looks terrific tonight."

Including the latest arrival, Lila thought. Pearl-gray sportcoat, charcoal slacks, a white shirt that looked as though it was made of silk, a muted tie that certainly was. For a garage mechanic, he certainly knew how to dress.

"Lila almost wore something besides that black dress she has on," Babs said. "And she looks so good in it, too."

"Won't get an argument from me on that." Bill pulled out his chair and sat down. "I was admiring it from across the room. There's something very provocative about black."

"Except at funerals," Eddie commented, and got a reproving frown from his wife. "What? What'd I say?"

"It didn't sound nice, sweetheart."

"Well, I didn't mean anything by it, dear."

"You should think before you speak, Eddie. Someone might take offense."

The wine steward arrived and Penny used the flurry of order-taking as a cover. "Bill said black is provocative, Lila," she murmured in a singsong tone. "I'll bet he's still interested."

"So?" Lila busied herself repositioning the forks beside her plate.

"You're hopeless," Penny said under her breath. Then she smiled at Bill and Jason. "Where have you two been keeping yourselves today? I haven't laid eyes on either of you once."

Jason blushed and put down his wineglass. "Well, I— that is, Danielle and I—you see, we—"

"Jason has met a wonderful young woman," Bill said, glancing with amusement at his son. "If I'd been a more understanding dad, I would have traded seating times with Danielle so they could sit together tonight."

Jason blushed more profusely. "No, Dad, I really didn't want you to do that. You and I are supposed to have dinner tonight. Danielle wouldn't hear of trading seats."

"As I said, a wonderful young woman." Bill glanced at Lila. "Amazingly perceptive."

Lila's heart pounded. Bill could have gracefully avoided having dinner with her by insisting Jason sit with his new girlfriend. Had she been in Bill's shoes, nursing a wounded ego, she would have done exactly that. Instead, Bill was here, undaunted, giving her, it seemed, one last chance to reconsider. The soup course arrived, but Lila wasn't even slightly hungry.

"Now we know where Jason's been all day," Penny said with a wink. "How about you, Bill?"

"Oh, I found a few guys who were interested in a friendly game of poker."

Eddie looked interested. "Oh, yeah? Are you gonna play again tonight?"

"Maybe." Bill's gaze flicked to Lila.

Eddie leaned forward. "If you do, I—" He paused as Babs nudged him. "Uh, I wish you luck."

"I could use it," Bill said.

"Have you been losing?" Babs asked as soup bowls gave way to salad plates.

"You could say that. But what the heck. Life's no fun if you don't take a gamble now and then," he said, looking meaningfully at Lila.

She noticed that he'd touched little of his soup or salad, and his wineglass was as full as when it was poured. "I've never been much of a gambler myself," she ventured. "I hate to lose."

"So I've heard." Bill caressed the stem of his wineglass with one finger.

Lila watched the movement and remembered the electricity of his touch. She gazed at the knot of his tie and longed to loosen it, to unbutton his shirt, to slip her hands inside. . . .

"But if you never gamble," Bill continued, his blue eyes focused on Lila, "you lose the chance to win. Winning's a real kick."

"Sure is," Eddie agreed. "Why, I remember one time, when I held four spades. But I kept my cool, and none of the guys suspected I was close to a straight. So then the last cards came up. You see, the dealer was over there, where Jason is, and I was where Babs is." Eddie cleared his throat and spread his hands. "Now picture the tension as the dealer starts to deal."

Lila couldn't concentrate as Eddie's story droned on endlessly and Bill continued to hold her gaze with his. The question was there between them as if it had been spoken. Slowly her silent answer formed. She wanted him more than she'd wanted anyone or anything in a long time. Did she have the courage to take what she wanted for once in her life?

Penny nudged her under the table, and she realized that her untouched salad plate had been replaced by a steaming prime rib dinner, and Eddie's tale of poker had finally come to a close. "Interesting story," she mumbled, smiling at Eddie.

"Eddie, I had no idea you were a gambler," Babs said, sounding less than thrilled.

"Well, I wouldn't, you know, jeopardize the household money, or anything," Eddie protested. "I'm not reckless. I'll bet you're not a serious gambler, either, are you, Bill?"

Bill's devil-may-care smile heated Lila's blood even more. "Depends on what's at stake, Eddie."

Eddie leaned back in a vain attempt to imitate Bill's confident attitude. "Well, yeah, I'd have to say that, too."

"Hey, Dad, you'd better eat some of that prime rib," Jason warned. "They're starting to clear the main course."

"So they are." He glanced at Lila's untouched meal and left his fork where it was. When the waiter appeared, Bill nodded for his plate to be taken away.

Penny put her napkin to her lips and muttered another message to Lila about never forgiving her if she blew this chance.

"Here it comes," Babs announced. "Baked Alaska. Look at those flames."

Lila watched the parade of waiters holding flaming trays of dessert over their heads as they crossed the dining room.

Bill put his napkin on the table. "Looks nice, but I'm really not a dessert eater," he said. "Think I'll take a turn around the deck." He gazed at Lila. "Care to join me?"

She panicked. This was it. Now or never. Her last chance.

"Go," Penny whispered under her breath.

Lila's heartbeat pounded in her ears so loudly she could barely hear her own voice agreeing to his invitation. When she stood, she had to grip the table to steady herself as she fought off a wave of lightheadedness. In seconds he was beside her, cupping her elbow, lending his support. She permitted him to guide her between the crowded tables and up the stairs. Too late she realized she hadn't said a word of farewell to the others at the table.

Bill steered her outside, and she drew the cool ocean breeze deep into her lungs.

"Congratulations," he said, slipping an arm around her waist.

"This may be the dumbest thing I've ever done in my life," she said as they walked along the deck.

"That makes two of us." He tightened his hold on her waist. "But as long as we've come this far, I think we'd better go below and find out for sure."

6

IN BILL'S CABIN drapes closed out the world; soft lights glowed above the headboard of the double bed, and the sheets lay open and smooth—a silent invitation. Lila had expected no less. The excitement she felt magnified every sensation—the easy rocking of the ship, the pulse of the ship's engines far below, the metallic click as Bill locked the door, the rustle of his sportcoat as he tossed it on a chair, the scent of his cologne as he came up behind her.

He brushed her hair aside and touched his lips to her skin. "Great dress," he murmured, kissing his way down her spine with a slow, measured pace that told her she was in the presence of a skilled lover.

Her breath came faster as he knelt and unfastened two buttons that snugged the dress at her waist. When he stood, he slipped both hands inside the loosened bodice. Pressing his palms against her ribs, he stroked slowly upward until he supported the weight of her breasts. "Perfect," he whispered, his breath warming the curve of her neck.

Her head lolled back against his shoulder and she closed her eyes. The friction of his calloused thumb against her nipple made her weak and liquid with desire.

"I love ripeness in a woman," he said, applying just enough pressure to her aching breasts that she sighed with relief. "You're so warm, so wonderfully warm, Lila. To think I almost missed touching you this way."

"I was . . . foolish." Lila formed her words with difficulty as his practiced caress robbed her of easy speech.

"Not foolish." His voice melted around her as he stroked her breasts until she vibrated with longing. "Cautious, that's all."

"Not anymore," she whispered.

"No. Not anymore." He slowly withdrew his hands and turned her to face him. "Now you're the woman I knew you could be. You should see your eyes. A man could go crazy looking into those eyes."

The seduction of his gaze pumped desire through her, leaving her dizzy. Trembling, she reached for the knot of his tie. "How about this man?"

"He's insane from wanting you."

She worked the tie loose and stripped it from under his collar. Then she reached for the top button of his shirt.

"Slowly, Lila," he cautioned. "Craziness makes it better."

"I know." She unfastened the next button.

"Yes. And you've wasted what you know on fools who can't appreciate. . . ." He sucked in his breath as her lips followed the path of her fingers, nibbling each exposed inch of skin. "Oh, Lila. . . ."

He tasted better than she'd imagined; the musky scent of him drove her wild. Her tongue made swirls in the mat of hair covering his chest, and she exulted in his shuddering response. But she would take it slow, as he'd asked, and build the tension in him as she knew he would in her. The reward of patience was pleasure. They had one night to create a work of lovemaking art they'd always remember. She eased the shirt from the waistband of his slacks and resisted stroking the fullness below his belt. Not yet.

He cradled her head and brought her lips back to his. "This is so good," he murmured against her mouth before dipping his tongue inside.

She arched upward and wrapped him in her arms, loving the solid feel of his chest against her breasts, the firmness of his groin settling into the hollow between her thighs. Knowing she would welcome him inside her as she now welcomed the thrust of his tongue, yet prolonging the moment before it happened, made her senses sing with anticipation.

He relinquished her mouth and reached for the shoulders of her dress. "I want this off, so I can feel you against me."

She straightened her arms while he peeled the material away, gradually exposing her breasts to his view. "You're spectacular." His gaze moved up to her face. "You have so much to offer a man, Lila. It's a shame that—"

She pressed her fingers to his lips. "No. Whatever you were going to say, the answer is no, it's not a shame. We're here tonight, and that's all that matters."

He let the top of her dress fall around her hips and lifted her hand to his lips. "You're right." He kissed the tip of each finger. "You're right," he said again, moving his caress to the inside of her wrist, her elbow, her bare shoulder. "Only a fool would have regrets at a feast like this." Cupping her breast in one hand, he leaned down and took the dusky tip in his mouth.

Lila tunneled her fingers through his hair and arched into his caress. He responded by nipping her gently with his teeth and she began to tremble. Patience was losing its charm. Desire grew less tame, less civilized, with every tug of his mouth at her breast. Her underclothes were drenched; the aching center of her womanhood throbbed with the need to be touched, to be filled. Before she could stop herself, she moaned aloud.

He raised his head to gaze deep into her eyes. "What a beautiful sound."

"I didn't think . . . I'd want you so much."

"It's a risk we both took."

"Feel how I'm shaking. I'm helpless."

He smiled. "Hardly, my love." He took her hand and placed it where his slacks strained to hold his passionate response to her. "Feel the power you have over me."

My love. The endearment had slipped from him as if he meant it. Although she had no business accepting it that way, she would for now. It sounded exactly right. With quivering fingers she unbuckled his belt and unfastened his slacks. The tempo of his breathing quickened as she drew the zipper down. She glanced into his eyes, questioning.

"Yes. Please, yes."

She eased his briefs down. He was magnificent, but she lacked the courage to praise him. Instead, she wrapped her fingers around the velvet shaft that she longed for, and heard his groan of pleasure. "For you, my love," she said softly, deliberately, as she stroked him. Touching him without begging for him to fill her took all her self-control, but she wanted him to need as much as she did.

His breathing grew ragged and his muscles tensed. "Stop," he said, grasping her wrist. "Just...stop. Could you—could you take off the rest of your things? I might . . . rip something." His expression was a mask of control but his eyes blazed with passion.

Lila smiled. He was definitely losing his restraint. She wasn't the only one consumed by need. Kicking off her shoes, she shimmied out of everything but her panties. She glanced at him and found him watching her with undisguised hunger.

"I've never wanted a woman the way I want you," he said. "Do you believe that?"

"Yes," she murmured, walking to the bed and stretching out on it. "Because I've never wanted anyone this much, either." The inside of her mouth grew moist as she focused on the gradual uncovering of male flesh while he undressed. She savored every revelation—the ripple of his thighs when he moved, the curve of his calf, the dimple in his buttocks when he turned away briefly to throw his clothes on the chair.

When at last he walked toward her, she felt an overpowering urge to tell him that she loved him, that somehow she knew this joining would be the most significant of her life. But of course she couldn't. Couldn't tell him and couldn't love him. This was about adult enjoyment, not sappy emotion. The agreement was silent, but clear.

"I love the way you look, lying there," he said.

"That's the idea," she replied softly.

He hesitated, as if to say more, but then he shook his head slightly and came toward her. "I love your ideas," he said, placing one knee on the bed and moving over her. She gazed up at him as he braced his arms on either side of her and looked into her eyes for a long time. "I pictured you like this so many times," he said at last.

"The reality far outshines my imagination. You are a glorious female for a man to have *under* him."

"Or *above* him," she teased gently.

"That, too. We'll try both, believe me. And anything else we can think of." He relaxed onto his elbows and touched one of her antique earrings. "You forgot these."

"You don't like making love to a woman wearing earrings?"

"I don't want anything on you or in you except me. This is my night and I want exclusive privileges."

"Then take them off."

"They're not hooked in?"

"No. They're very old, and they just clip on. Take them off."

He carefully pulled one away and kissed her bare earlobe. "That's better. Now I can do this," he said, circling the curve of her ear with his tongue.

"Mmm." Her skin flushed at even this most delicate of touches. Apparently he could arouse her by caressing her anywhere.

He removed the other earring and she heard them rattle on the nightstand before she became oblivious to anything but the movement of his lips and tongue. He nipped and nibbled from her throat to her breasts and lower, finally pulling away the barrier of her panties to bestow the ultimate intimacy. She writhed in his arms, abandoning herself to this man who so knowingly teased and sweetly tortured her into mindless physical joy.

He returned to kiss her lips while his hands roamed over her heated body and kept her constantly on the brink of release without driving her over. "Happy?" he murmured as she whimpered and dug her fingers into his shoulder.

"Delirious," she gasped.

"Me, too," he whispered, before capturing her mouth for a deep and compelling kiss.

She was dazed with passion by the time he reached into the drawer of the nightstand and sheathed himself. When she realized that at last she would have what she'd longed for, in her frenzy had even begged for, she grew still and her heart pounded frantically as he turned back to her.

"What is it?" he crooned, stroking her flushed cheek. "You look scared."

"I am."

"You don't have to be, Lila. I sure as hell won't hurt you. Is there something I should know? Something about this that gives you pain?"

"No."

"Then what?" He gently parted her thighs and stroked her moist flesh. "You're so ready, Lila." He smiled. "And you've asked me a few times."

"I'm afraid . . . that I'll never be the same," she stammered. "I want you so much I can barely stand it, and still I'm afraid . . ."

"Risk it, Lila." He moved over her and parted her thighs. "Don't give up on me now."

She gazed up at him and the fire in his eyes fueled the ache deep within her. She didn't resist as he probed and found her easily. As he'd said, her body was ready. More than ready. Pulsing. Demanding the first thrust that he postponed while he waited, his gaze intense.

Beads of sweat stood out on his forehead as he held himself back, poised. "Lila." His voice was rough. "Tell me what you want."

"You," she said, and lifted her hips to meet him as he pushed forward with an exultant cry.

"Oh," she sighed as he burrowed deep. She hadn't been wrong about the risk. This feeling of completion, of rightness, was glorious . . . and filled with danger.

He didn't give her time to think more than that before he eased back and plunged forward again, sending pleasure signals all through her body. He'd done his preliminary work well, and she was dynamite on a very short fuse.

His next thrust made her gasp and arch her back.

"That's my girl," he whispered in her ear. "Show me what you're made of," he urged, sliding in tight to put exquisite pressure on the perfect spot.

She moaned and wrapped her legs around his.

"That's right. Get all you can." He pumped slowly, forcefully as the spring within her tightened to a red-hot coil. He kept up the rhythm with instinctive persistence until the spring released. Crying out his name, she rocked with the convulsions he'd orchestrated with such finesse.

"Good," he murmured, rocking with her. "Good, Lila. So good." He gasped as the needs of his body claimed him at last and his movements picked up momentum.

Lila felt open as never before, as if no man had ever before delved this deep. She welcomed him as if she were parting layers of her soul, more with each thrust, until at last he surged forward on a cry of completion and she felt him pulse within her. Wrapping her arms tightly around him, she wondered if he'd lost himself as thoroughly as she'd lost herself this fateful night; would he dare tell her if he had?

BILL LAY QUIETLY, savoring the plumpness of her breasts rising and falling beneath him as her breathing gradually slowed to normal. She'd really blown him away, and they hadn't tried anything more daring than traditional lovemaking. She was a fabulous lover. He'd never had sex like this the first time with anyone. Except for that one glitch, when she temporarily got scared, she'd been the most responsive partner he'd ever met—and wow, what pleasure. To think they hadn't even explored all the possibilities of lovemaking, the fun variations. One night. One short night. Damn.

He'd told himself they'd be far better off if they didn't see each other again after the ship docked. The plan seemed like a stupid one now that he knew what he'd be giving up in the morning. The ship was going fast, too. He could tell by the tempo of the engines and the sway of the cabin that this barge was cooking, taking him and Lila to a parting of the ways on the double. Short of sabotaging the engine room and leaving them all to drift around for a while, he wasn't sure what to do about it, either.

Not that he was getting carried away; he still didn't want any kind of commitment. But he sure could do with a few more nights like this one. She was wonderful company outside the bedroom, too. He hadn't found too many women of that kind in the past. No doubt about it, Lila was the most satisfying lady to cross his path in years, and he'd be a fool to let the end of the cruise put a halt to everything. He was getting older, but apparently not much smarter.

She stirred beneath him and he raised his head from the cradle of her shoulder. "Am I too heavy?" he asked, looking into eyes misty with satisfaction.

"No, you feel nice."

He smiled. Her voice had the husky sound of a woman who's just made love. He enjoyed the music of it. "You feel nice, too." He stroked the curve of her hip and eased into the damp site of their joining. "But I suppose I should tend to a few things," he added. As he withdrew, he felt as if he were leaving paradise.

In the bathroom he gazed into the mirror. *You look like a love-struck fool,* he thought, *with that silly grin on your face.* Well, he wouldn't let himself be love-struck, even if he looked that way. She was fun to be with, a passionate lover, but that was it, right? He pushed away the memory of the way his heart had tightened when he walked toward her as she lay on the bed, and of the insane rantings of his mind when he was loving her, toward the end, and she'd really opened up. He'd damned near told her he loved her then. What a mistake that would have been.

Okay, so he wasn't going to fall in love, or anything crazy like that, but maybe he could explore the chances of seeing her again, after the ship docked. Maybe he could work around to the subject with some small talk.

He left the bathroom and walked back to the bed. She hadn't covered up, and he liked that—liked it so much he wanted to join her and start all over again. "Since we missed dinner, would you like to order something from the galley?" he asked.

But when she stretched languorously, he almost lost his interest in food. "Sure," she said, rolling to her side. "Maybe just sandwiches."

"And a bottle of wine," he suggested.

"Why not? Let's live a little."

He sat on the bed and picked up the telephone receiver. "I think that's what we've been doing," he said, leaning down to give her a kiss. The kiss turned into more than he'd bargained for and the man answering the telephone in the galley had to speak twice before Bill could extricate himself and give their order.

"How long?" she asked.

Boy, was she turning into a vamp. He knew exactly why she'd asked. "Not long enough," he said, sliding into bed with her and winding their bodies together. "We'll have to control ourselves, and one of us may have to put a few articles of clothing on to answer the door."

"Too bad."

"You're telling me. Maybe this meal wasn't such a good idea."

"Yes, it was." She snuggled against him. "We have to keep up our strength."

"Good point. Lila, I don't think I mentioned that you're the most fantastic—"

"You'd better change the subject," she interrupted, nudging his stiffening member with her thigh, "or we'll never answer the door."

"You could be right about that." He rolled her onto her back. "But I can't think of any other subjects."

"Tell me about your racing."

He shook his head. "It's just a hobby. Tell me about your job."

"Ugh. Not now."

"Your kids, then. You've met mine, the one and only. What about your daughters?"

She sighed. "Talking about them will certainly dampen our romantic spirits."

"We can recover, after the food's delivered."

"Okay. First of all, I love Tracey and Sarah to death, but—"

"But they're driving you up the wall," he guessed.

"Yep. Sarah's at Bryn Mawr, where she begged to go, and she's liable to flunk out and waste all that money I've paid to send her. They don't give refunds on college tuitions, you know."

"Make her pay it back to you," Bill suggested.

"Doing what? The girl's never held a job."

"So? Fast-food chains are always hiring."

"Well, I—" Lila paused. "I have visions of her working at a fast-food place forever, I guess, if she quits school now."

"Seems like that's her choice, not yours."

Lila frowned and put some distance between them. "You can afford to be cavalier about this. Jason's safely graduated and on his way to a good job back East. Whereas my two—"

"You're right." Bill sensed he'd strayed too far into forbidden territory. "I have no business making suggestions or passing judgment."

"Bill," she began softly, hesitating, "this sort of discussion could ruin tonight. Let's not get tangled up in each other's problems. By this time in our lives we've nearly finished raising our children—probably with different methods that we'll defend to anyone who challenges them."

"Probably," he agreed. She was wise, too, it seemed.

"And we have strong opinions about other things, opinions we won't readily change, at least not as readily as a twenty-year-old might."

He grinned, wanting to lighten her up. "You mean we're old fogies stuck in our ways?"

She blinked. "That's pretty blunt."

"It was meant to make you laugh. Come here, Lila." He gathered her close. "Let's not spoil the magic of what we've just shared. You're probably right that our personalities are very definitely set, that they may not mesh as easily as they might have when we were twenty years younger. But Lila, we sure meshed like bandits not half an hour ago." He was relieved to see the dreamy light return to her eyes.

"We did, didn't we?"

He brushed a strand of hair from her cheek. "Do you think there's any way we could get together, just once in a while, after this cruise?" He waited with held breath.

"What do you mean?"

He expelled the breath. At least she was willing to talk about it. "Eighty miles isn't so far. I could drive down, or you could drive up. Just . . . occasionally."

"You mean to spend the night."

He chuckled. "I don't mean to catch a movie."

"Because the sex is good."

"More than good, but don't make me out to be that crass. As the cliché goes, I like you as a person, too. Plus I think you like me." He gazed into her eyes and his voice gentled. "If we didn't care about each other as people, we wouldn't have experienced such joy in making love. We haven't engaged in mindless coupling. Not by a long shot." He watched her expression as she mulled over his suggestion. He could see she was torn.

"I don't think it would work," she said at last. "Much as I'd love to say it would so that I could look forward to more nights like this."

"Why wouldn't it work? Consider it the way you would . . ." He fished around for an analogy. "A club meeting," he finished.

That made her laugh. "An organization for the promotion of mutual sexual pleasure?"

"Right. An exclusive club, just for you and me." Maybe he could get her with cleverness. "In fact, we'll call it SPOT, Sexual Pleasure Organization for Two."

"With club rules?"

"Sure. Club rules. We'll—" He paused as a knock sounded at the door. "Dinner," he said, scrambling from the bed and into his pants. "We'll continue this in a minute."

To protect Lila from embarrassment, Bill kept the steward who'd brought the tray outside the cabin. He suspected she wouldn't be thrilled to have a stranger in the room when she was lying in bed naked, no matter how many covers she pulled over herself.

"Here we go," he said, carrying the tray in himself and placing it on the bed.

"You're a thoughtful guy," she said, sliding out from under the sheets. "Some men might have shown me off to the steward as if I were a trophy. You know—'look what I have in my bed.'"

"The same ones who worry about their laundry, no doubt," said Bill, pouring her a glass of wine from the chilled bottle. "You've got to stay away from those guys, Lila. Stick with the club."

"Bill, you're great, but—"

"I always hate sentences that start that way. Here." He handed her the glass and poured one for himself. "To SPOT. An idea whose time has come."

"I can't drink to that, Bill. I'm sorry, but I'm not ready for SPOT."

He lowered his glass. Damn, she was slipping away from him right when he thought they had a deal. "Why not?"

"My daughter and grandchild live with me, for one thing. I don't entertain men overnight and I don't stay out all night at their places, either."

He didn't like the sound of her restrictive living arrangements. Not one bit. He felt judgment rising in him again and he fought to subdue it. "Does your daughter have a husband?"

"They're separated."

"Legally?"

"No papers have been filed, if that's what you mean."

"That's what I mean," Bill said, as his dreams faded before his eyes. This woman, luscious though she was, seemed pretty well tangled up with her kids. "A legal separation would obligate your daughter's husband to give financial support and you wouldn't have to do it, which I assume you are doing."

"Yes, I am." The belligerent look returned to her eyes. "Tracey has a ten-month-old baby and an unhappy marriage, that she thinks she'll have no chance of saving if she files separation papers. She's hoping this separation will give them each time to appreciate each other more."

"That's not a bad idea, but you're the one who's in-convenienced in the meantime."

"Not unless I'm trying to carry on a love affair," she shot back.

He noticed the tense set of her shoulders, her white knuckles as she gripped the stem of the wineglass. He glanced down to discover he was clutching his glass with equal force. A few more exchanges like this one and they'd destroy what precious hours they had left, not to mention any chance of other meetings. "Time-out," he said, forcing himself to relax, to give up the fight.

"We're doing it again, aren't we?"

"You're not. I am," he admitted. "We have tonight, and now I'm greedy for more. In the process of trying for more, I keep getting caught in the very quicksand you've warned me about. It's not your doing; it's mine, and I'll stop now. Morning is creeping closer, and we have better things to do than argue away our remaining moments together."

Her smile was slow in coming, but it came. "I'll drink to that," she said.

He touched the rim of her glass with his. "To de-lights of the flesh." He boldly swept his gaze over her body and took satisfaction in the rosy flush that soon touched every visible inch of her. No matter what had been said, it was obvious she still wanted him.

7

"THAT WAS BY FAR the best food I've eaten on this cruise," Lila proclaimed, wiping her fingers on a napkin.

"And the best wine?" Bill prompted.

"And the best wine," she agreed.

"Think how the vacation would have improved if we'd done this earlier." He topped off her wineglass.

Lila leaned against the headboard and stretched out her uncovered legs. "Yes, I've thought of that, too. Especially because I feel so comfortable with you." She glanced at him over the rim of her glass. "You'd probably be surprised to know how shy I am, usually."

"I wouldn't be surprised at all." Bill moved the tray over to the dresser before stripping off his pants. "Matter of fact, I wondered if you'd be really shy at first."

She smiled as he walked toward her, totally unselfconscious, his body already reacting to the promise of more lovemaking. "I can't imagine a woman being shy with you. You behave as if modesty is a waste of time."

He grinned and joined her on the bed. "Isn't it?"

"Certainly in this case."

"Then if you feel so comfortable, let's play." He dipped his finger into her wineglass and stroked the liquid over her nipple. "Not that you don't taste wonderful all by yourself, but I've always wanted . . ."

Lila's breathing quickened as he leaned down and sucked gently. "Bill—I might drop this glass," she warned as her muscles grew lazy and fluid.

He lifted his head. "Here," he murmured, taking it from her limp fingers and setting it beside them on the nightstand. "Now lie down and close your eyes."

She followed his instructions and soon felt as if she were an artist's canvas as he created damp patterns on her skin.

"This is a little-known beauty treatment," he said, licking the moisture from her breasts and the hollow of her throat. He dipped each of her fingers into the wine and drew them one by one into his mouth.

Her excitement mounted as he kissed his way down to her navel and scooped out the wine pooled there with swirls of his tongue. She was damp with more than wine by the time he stroked wine over her thighs, and at last, between her legs. When his mouth found her, she gasped at the intensity of her pleasure.

He settled in as if to stay, and stay he did, until the pleasure had grown beyond all her attempts to contain it. Begging him to stop so that they could share the ecstasy, she writhed beneath his grip and learned the measure of his strength and determination. He would not stop; he would give her this, and finally, in a waterfall of sensation, she took what he offered.

When her convulsions ebbed away, he slid up beside her and gazed into her face. "Wine will never be that good again," he whispered, kissing her.

The taste of passion on his lips stirred her anew. "I can't believe it," she murmured against his mouth. "I still want you, after all that."

"The miracle of a woman," he said, slipping his fingers into her moistness and finding her vulnerable spot. "I'm envious. You'll be able to crowd so much more into these hours."

She was stunned that he could build a response again, so soon. "Believe me . . . I'm not usually . . ."

"Shh," he whispered, kissing her cheeks, her eyes, her mouth. "You are now. Enjoy."

Enjoy she did. In the hours before dawn he pleasured her as no man had ever done before. She had stumbled unwittingly upon mature sensuality in this cabin. The last years of her marriage had been less than exotic sexually, and since her divorce she'd entered into two brief and uninspiring affairs that had left her convinced she would live the rest of her life alone and untouched.

She thought she'd accepted the end of her sexual life, yet apparently she hadn't, not fully. Subconscious drives had prompted her to buy the red dress, and after it, the black. Even at their first meeting, Bill had sensed her restlessness, and her unacknowledged quest for fulfillment had proved a powerful aphrodisiac.

All through the delicious hours, she fought drowsiness whenever it threatened to rob her of new sensations and fascinating exploration. Bill laughingly offered to order coffee to keep them awake. Yet eventually they lay quietly, exhausted by the powerful experiences they'd shared and lulled by the drone of the ship's engines. They sprawled across the bunched sheets, facing each other, eyelids heavy, lips smiling. Bill's leg, coarse with hair, rested atop Lila's smooth calf; his large, blunt fingers covered her slender, tapered ones. Gradually their eyes closed . . . and they slept.

A SOFT BUMP as the ship nudged into the wharf prodded Lila awake. She opened her eyes slowly. Across from her Bill slept, his bristly morning face relaxed, his piercing blue eyes shuttered. Tenderness and gratitude brought a lump to her throat. He'd given her so much.

She sorted through her memories of the night as if handling cherished pieces of jewelry preserved in a velvet-lined chest. She hadn't guessed when the evening began that he would cover her in precious gems of sensation, decorating her until she believed in her own beauty. Nor had she fathomed what she'd lose when dawn arrived. Now she knew.

Yet she was afraid to grasp this happiness for fear it would disintegrate like cotton candy in the heat of her grip. They'd nearly quarreled about each of her daughters. She didn't doubt there were aspects of Bill's life, aspects of which she knew nothing, that would bother her as well. And both of them were beyond the age when it was easy to reshape habits and beliefs to suit a loved one.

Loved one. Lila tested the phrase as she studied Bill's sleeping face, his strong arms and gentle hands. The sheet was draped across his waist, covering the rest of him, but she knew that part intimately, too, and had rejoiced in it many times in the past few hours. Physically she knew Bill better than she'd known any other man, even Stan, and she loved what she'd learned. But that didn't constitute loving Bill. Huge gaps remained in her knowledge of his moods, his habits, his way of life. Love meant understanding and accepting facets of his life she'd never experienced.

A younger woman might have called what she felt love, but Lila, dazzled as she was, couldn't. She and Bill weren't in love—not yet—and to explore that possibility might destroy the magic they'd found. Her original decision had been wise and she'd stay with it. When she left this room, she and Bill would return to the status of strangers.

Noises drifted into the cabin from the deck and hallway as passengers hurried to their last breakfast aboard ship or rushed to buy souvenirs from the gift shop. Lila knew she'd have to leave soon. She hadn't packed. Still, she lay quietly, unwilling to give up the last moments of gazing at Bill.

Eventually the bustling and laughter aboard the ship woke him. His gaze was dreamy as he focused on Lila and he smiled, but soon the smile faded and regret lurked in his eyes. "I don't want this to end," he said, his voice scratchy from sleep.

"I don't want this to be spoiled," she countered softly. "We've been drifting in never-never land, but the real world is on the other side of the gangplank. What we've had might die, like some exotic bloom, if we tried to transplant it to our everyday lives."

"That's one point of view."

"Bill, I don't want to take the chance. These hours have been too special. I couldn't bear to have them tarnished by the humdrum of daily life."

He circled her waist with one arm. "Come closer and tell me that."

She resisted his pull. "I have to go."

"Then kiss me goodbye," he said, urging her nearer.

"When I'm dressed. When I'm about to leave." She struggled away from him and swung her legs over the edge of the bed.

He grasped her wrist. "Lila, just once more. We have time. Don't go without—"

"I must." She stood and he released her arm. She didn't dare tell him that making love once more might destroy all her carefully constructed logic. She had to get out of that cabin, and fast. She gathered her clothes from the floor and began putting them on.

"Did I tell you that you have the most beautiful breasts I've ever touched?"

She glanced at him and found him watching her with his head propped on his hand. "I don't think so, but...thanks." She pulled the black dress over her hips and slipped her arms into the sleeves.

"Wait. Don't—"

"Bill, this is what we decided. It's for the best." She reached behind her back and fastened the two buttons holding the dress snug. Then she turned away from him, hiding the thrust of her pouting nipples through the fabric. Better he not know the effect his entreaties had on her.

"That's what I thought, too," he said, "until this moment. Now I'm greedy, Lila. I can't accept the idea that I'll never make love to you again."

"That's because I'm still here, in this room." She searched through her clutch bag for her comb and stepped into the bathroom to drag her hair into some order. She'd feel conspicuous enough walking the ship's hallways in last night's evening dress without having her hair in tangles, too. "Once I'm gone the urge will disappear," she said, praying she was right, for her sake and his.

She washed her face and patted it dry. Amazing, she thought, how wonderful she looked after a night of virtually no sleep. A night with Bill apparently was more therapeutic than a beauty mask. She left the bathroom and stood facing the bed. "I guess that's it, then."

"You're radiant," he murmured, gazing at her. "You would have helped me a lot if you could have managed to look haggard."

"Bill . . ." She fingered the clasp on her purse. "Last night was the most . . . I've never even come close to having. . . . Damn, I'm stumbling around this. But you gave me the most astounding—"

"Never mind," he said gently. "I know what you mean. The same goes for me."

She shook her head. "It can't be the same for you. I can sense that your experience is much wider than mine."

"Maybe wider, but no deeper. Last night was the best, Lila. No contest."

Tears misted her eyes. "Thank you." She'd needed so much to hear that. She'd believe it was true, and that truth would be the final jewel in her chest of memories. She approached the bed. "Goodbye, Bill."

He gazed at her silently. "You're sure?" His voice was husky.

She nodded, and leaned down to brush her lips against his. She straightened immediately, not trusting herself to give him a deeper kiss.

"I'll never forget you," he said.

"Nor I you." She held his gaze for a moment longer before turning and walking quickly toward the door. She unlocked it and left without looking back.

"IT WAS THE MOST WONDERFUL night of your life and you're never going to see him again." Penny leaned back in the passenger seat of Lila's sedan as they left the docks and headed for the freeway. "Pardon me, lady, but you're crazier than I thought."

There had been little time for talking once Lila had returned to her cabin. Since she had to be back in La Jolla for a noon appointment, she'd packed in record time and she and Penny had hurried down the gangplank. Their haste had put them well ahead of Bill and Jason, she'd concluded with relief when she hadn't seen them in the line of passengers at the customs desk.

But now she and Penny were in the car and set for an hour's drive. Penny's quest for information couldn't be deflected any longer.

"Look, that was the idea going into this," Lila explained. "Neither of us wanted any loose ends to clutter up our lives."

"Well, yeah, if you'd had an ordinary roll in the hay. But from what little you've told me, this was special. And I'm insanely jealous, by the way. We'll get that out of the way right quick."

Lila smiled. "Okay."

"But just because I'm jealous doesn't mean I don't want to hear about it. Vicarious thrills are better than no thrills at all."

Lila kept her eyes on the road. Just thinking about last night raised her temperature. Talking about it might make her drive into a ditch.

"Lila Kedge, your cheeks are positively rosy! My goodness, I've never seen you this way over a man."

"Penny, I had no idea that I could be so . . . so uninhibited."

"Yeah? Like how?"

Lila shook her head, her cheeks aflame. "Now, when he's not here, I can't even tell you without feeling embarrassed, but with him, I lost all my shyness. I can't explain it."

"*I* can. You, romantic klutz that you are, somehow stumbled upon the best darn lover in Southern California, that's what, and you're letting him get away. Couldn't you at least have slipped my phone number into his suitcase when he wasn't looking?"

"Probably a lot of what happened between us had to do with the cruise," Lila mused, not really listening to Penny. "Away from that environment we'd be ordinary people making ordinary love."

"B.S."

"And if we tried to drag it out, eventually we'd tire of each other and look for some graceful way out. This way we cut clean, with nothing but wonderful memories of what happened between us."

"Did he agree to all that horse hockey?"

"Well, sort of. Not exactly," Lila admitted.

"He didn't! Because he's not the lily-livered, chickenhearted disgrace to his gender that you are. Lila, I'm so put out with you that you didn't grab that man by whatever was handy and hang on for dear life."

"Penny, just because that's what you want doesn't mean that I—"

"And what about the red dress? What about the *backless* black dress? You started out to catch yourself a big one, and then when you did, you got scared and threw him back. You'll regret this day. Mark my words."

Lila sighed. "Well, it doesn't matter now. The whole episode is over."

"I'm sure it is. When some man gives you all he's got and you still say no thanks, he won't be back for another blow to his ego. Damn, I wish he had my phone number."

Lila glanced at her friend. "I'm sorry this cruise didn't work out better for you. All that money spent and you came up empty."

"Yeah, well, I learned a lot the past few days, though." Penny chuckled. "And the most important thing I learned was never to take you on a husband-hunting trip again."

THE PLUM-COLORED JAGUAR XJ6 rose on the lift's pedestal until the wire-rimmed wheels were even with Bill's chest. "I think we'd better check the brake shoes, Henry," he said, prying gently at the wire rims to get to the lug nuts.

"Yeah, I think it's the shoes," his customer agreed. "Just a little too much squeal for my taste. So, how was the cruise? You just got back this morning, right?"

"That's right." Bill picked up the air gun and attacked the lug nuts. Henry liked to stay and talk while the work was being done. Ordinarily Bill didn't mind, but he didn't feel like discussing the cruise.

"Any good-looking broads, or were they all old and dried up?"

Bill paused and glanced at Henry. Couldn't offend the guy. He was too good a customer and knew too many people in Mission Viejo. "What do you think?" he asked with a grin.

Henry chuckled. "I think you got a little. Am I right?"

Bill just smiled and returned to the lug nuts.

"I shoulda known you would, you alley cat. Did you con them with some line about what a fancy driver you are? Offer to show them your trophies when you get home?"

Bill loosened the last nut and eased off the wheel. "Nope."

"Come on, I'll bet you did. Women eat that stuff up. I'll bet you bragged about the time you almost fried in that wreck—worked on their sympathy. Admit it. You race to get the chicks."

"Well, it doesn't hurt my standing any, if that's what you mean." Bill leaned the tire against the garage wall and returned to examine the brake shoe.

" 'Doesn't hurt my standing,' he says." Henry barked with laughter. "I've seen them crowding around the pits. Listen, if I suddenly ended up single, I'd buy me a race car in a minute. As things are now, Louise wouldn't hear of it. I keep telling her that lots of the guys in these amateur races are in their fifties, but she thinks I'm too old to start playing Mario Andretti."

Bill turned to him. "Do you really want to race?"

"Sure! I think it'd be a kick."

"Then do it."

Henry clapped him on the shoulder. "Obviously you've forgotten what it's like to be married. Louise would make my life miserable."

Bill was silent, not sure what to say. It was Henry's marriage, not his.

"Yeah, yeah, I know," Henry said, mistaking Bill's silence for censure. "I should stand up to her, but at our age it's hardly worth it. Racing cars isn't an issue to get divorced over, you know?"

Bill nodded. "You're right. It's not." He wouldn't have crossed Joan on that one, either. Fate had given him more freedom, but he wouldn't have chosen divorce in order to race cars and live as he liked. But now that he had it, he wouldn't trade that freedom away, either.

"So anyway, this woman from the cruise—you'll be seeing her again?"

"Nope." Bill forced a grin and turned back to the disc brakes. "Shipboard romance."

"You sly sonofabitch. Damn, what I wouldn't give to be you for a week. I'm happy with Louise, but your life is so . . . I don't know . . . you have all these opportunities. Was she great, huh? I'll bet she was great."

"These brake shoes could go a little longer, Henry. They're not really bad yet."

"Not talking, are you? I'll bet she was something, then, because you'd tell me if she was a dog. I know you."

No, you don't, not by a long shot, Bill thought. *Or you'd recognize the pain behind all this bull I'm giving you.* He smiled and pointed at the brake shoes. "Want to leave them on?"

"Nah. Let's change them. Besides, I wanted to ask you about that last race. I wasn't sure what happened in the final turn, when it looked as though you'd nosed out that number six car."

Bill understood Henry's decision. Henry's money allowed him to schedule unnecessary repairs when it served his purpose. In this case, along with the repairs, he wanted a chance to talk racing and women with Bill. Several of Bill's customers were attracted to the idea of having their cars worked on by a race car driver; it improved their self-image. Bill didn't mind. He loved to race, and if it helped business, so much the better. He was willing to talk all Henry wanted about racing. It was the discussion of Lila that he'd just as soon avoid.

"That guy in the number six car was a mean sucker," Bill said, preparing to remove the other wheels on the Jag. "He bumped me about every chance he got, so finally I nudged him a little."

"So I figured." Henry looked at Bill with admiration. "You're no pansy, Windsor. That's why I like watching you race. That little 'Vette is a beauty, too. That baby can sure go. Did you and the guys work out that problem with the carburetor?"

Bill nodded and proceeded to explain the recent modifications to his race car. He turned to the subject with relief. It took his mind off Lila and the wrenching in his gut every time he remembered those last moments in his cabin.

With their conversation about racing and Bill's sluggishness after having had very little sleep the night before, the brake job took the rest of the afternoon. Finally, Bill wiped off his hands. "That should keep you awhile, Henry."

"Appreciate it, Bill. Say, how's that son of yours? Didn't he go on the cruise with you?"

Bill laughed. "We started out together, but as soon as he met a gorgeous redhead we didn't see much of each other."

Henry winked. "A chip off the old block, huh?"

"I don't know. He might get serious and marry this one. He's in Anaheim meeting her folks. He'll have to work fast, though. He's due in Boston in five days."

"Ah, if he's anything like his old man, he'll forget that wedding bells stuff for a while. No need to get tied down too soon, right?"

Bill shrugged. "I guess that's up to Jason."

"Yeah, well, tell him old Henry said to sow some wild oats, test out the girls back East first."

"I'll tell him."

"See you at the next race, Bill."

"Right."

At last Henry left in the shiny Jag. Bill straightened up the shop, a chore he loved. He wiped down the hand tools and put them away, wound up cords and swept the cement floor. He prided himself on keeping a clean shop. Customers had spread the word that you didn't end up with greasy handprints on the hood or oil stains on the carpet when you had Bill Windsor handle the job.

As he drove home he realized that except for the time Henry had brought up the subject, he hadn't thought of Lila while he'd been working on the Jag. Thank God his work still had the power to absorb him so thoroughly.

He wished Jason had come home from the cruise with him instead of deciding to visit Danielle's parents. The house would be mighty empty tonight. He pulled into the driveway of the mission-style home and the garage door slid up to welcome him. That would be the extent of his welcome, too, he thought.

The house barely looked lived in. The maid had been there in his absence. Usually he liked order and quiet,

You may be the winner of the

MILLION DOLLAR GRAND PRIZE!

This lovely Victorian pewter-finish miniature is perfect for displaying a treasured photograph. And it's yours FREE as added thanks for giving our Reader Service a try!

DETACH AND MAIL TODAY

Business Reply Mail
No Postage Stamp
Necessary if Mailed
in Canada

Postage will be paid by

HARLEQUIN READER SERVICE®
P.O. BOX 609
FORT ERIE, ONTARIO
L2A 9Z9

Canada Post
Postes Canada
125

but tonight the place felt like a tomb. He switched on the television just to hear some voices and climbed the stairs to the master suite. At least here there was a certain disorder; he hadn't unpacked anything except his shaving kit. He'd done that much before leaving for the shop because he wanted to look again at the earrings he'd picked up from his nightstand aboard ship.

Now they winked at him from the bathroom counter as he washed up. Lila had been very clear about not wanting to see him again. She'd made quite a speech about how contacting each other after they left the ship could ruin what they'd shared. Yet she'd left the earrings behind. They looked expensive. Something had to be done about them.

He'd read about people who deliberately forgot to take all their belongings with them, subconsciously creating an excuse to renew the contact they'd broken. He'd love to believe that was Lila's motivation. He'd soon know if it was.

8

As STEVIE WAILED in a back bedroom and the cats wound around Lila's ankles begging for dinner, she massaged her temples and wondered if it had been only that morning that she'd told Bill goodbye. "Tracey, honey, can you do something for Stevie?" she called to her daughter who was watching television in the living room.

"I don't know what he wants," Tracey called back. "I've fed him, changed his diaper, and rocked him. He should go to sleep in a bit."

"He's teething," Lila reminded her daughter. "He might need some of that numbing stuff rubbed on his gums."

"I did that, Mom. Just relax. He'll stop in a minute."

Lila tried to block out the crying but couldn't. She'd lost that ability sometime after her own babies grew up. Now the plaintive wails were driving her to distraction. She dumped dry food into two dishes for the cats and went back to Stevie's room. Not really Stevie's room, but Sarah's, she amended to herself. If Sarah flunked out this term and came home, Stevie would be moved into Lila's office, an unappealing scenario.

Stevie was on his knees, clutching the crib railing like a prisoner behind bars. He stopped crying when he saw Lila. As she approached the crib, he held up both arms.

"What is it, sweetheart?" She scooped him up and he grabbed on tight. The front of his sleeper was damp with tears but otherwise he was dry and smelled talcum-powder sweet. Bill had called this move of Tracey's an inconvenience, and it was, she supposed. Yet she loved the way Stevie trusted her, a trust born of proximity. Two months ago when Tracey had arrived, he'd been restless and fearful in Lila's arms. Not now.

"I guess you're lonesome," she crooned, pacing in front of the crib while she rubbed his back. Tracey had told her that such behavior would only spoil him. Lila had observed that she and her daughter had patience in different areas where Stevie was concerned. Tracey had the patience to let him cry out his displeasure at going to bed; Lila had the patience to soothe it away. More than once Lila had opened her mouth to offer advice on child-raising, but each time she'd thought better of it. Consequently, she and Tracey got along moderately well.

When Stevie stopped crying, Lila could hear the ocean crashing against the rocks at the base of the cliff. Closed windows muted the sound into a lullaby, and gradually Stevie relaxed and rested his curly head on her shoulder. Too late she realized that he'd probably drool on her good lavender suit, but the peace she'd created by picking him up and walking with him was worth it.

Lila cursed silently when the telephone broke the silence. Stevie jerked upright and he tensed. All her efforts swirled down the drain; he was wide awake.

"It's okay. Go back to sleep," she murmured, willing Tracey to pick up the phone quickly. It was probably that idiot husband of hers. Mike and his typically poor timing. The ringing stopped and Lila resumed her walking and rubbing.

"Mom?" In the doorway, Tracey's silhouette shimmered with a golden halo where the hall light touched the edges of her long blond hair. "You in here?"

Stevie whipped around at the sound of his mother's voice and called out a syllable approximating "Ma."

"I was trying to get him to sleep," Lila said pointedly.

"Oh, just put him in the crib, Mom. He'll think he needs that kind of attention all the time. Besides, the phone's for you. I think it's long distance."

"Tracey, if you'd just walk him for a while and settle him down," Lila began, breaking her self-imposed rule about motherly advice.

"Mother, I know Stevie. He'll tyrannize you if you give him a chance. Just put him in the crib." She flipped her hair back over her shoulders. "Better yet, I'll do it."

"He'll just cry," Lila warned, relinquishing the baby.

"That's because he hasn't learned how to swear yet," Tracey said, settling Stevie into the crib. He began to wail immediately.

"Tracey—"

"Answer your call, Mom. Might be somebody wanting a five-million-dollar house."

Lila sighed and left the room, nearly stumbling over Onyx, her coal-black cat, who had come to see where all the people were. Lila headed for her office and shut the door. She wondered if her life had always been this hectic, or if the contrast—coming straight home from the cruise ship this morning—was making it seem more stressful than usual.

She picked up the tail of the Garfield desk phone her daughters had given her last Christmas, and the plastic cat's eyes opened. "Hello?" she said, meeting Garfield's worldly stare.

"Hello, Lila."

"Bill." Her pulse raced and she lowered herself into her desk chair. This was all she needed to send her to the funny farm. "What—"

"I called about your earrings."

"Oh."

"Did you realize you left them?"

"Yes, when I changed clothes in my cabin. But I thought it would be . . . awkward to try and get them back." Stevie's crying penetrated through the wall and Onyx scratched at the door, wanting in. "I assumed you'd turn them over to the staff if you found them."

"I considered it."

His voice aroused all the emotions she'd been tamping down since morning—longing, sadness, desire. "Why didn't you?"

"Because you might have left them on purpose."

"Of course not. I simply forgot, in the rush of dressing, of leaving—"

"Maybe you didn't mean to leave them, but it could have been a subconscious wish on your part. People often leave behind objects that must be returned, and—"

"You're making a case where there is none, Bill." Her reply was firm; her conscience prickled. Maybe he was right, but she couldn't let him know.

"Okay. It's your call. The earrings seem valuable, and I hate to trust them to the mail. I have some business in

La Jolla this weekend, anyway. If you'll give me your address, I'll drop them by."

"No!" Lila panicked. While he was safely in Mission Viejo, she'd be fine. Face-to-face with him, she might weaken. She might. . . .

"Then what do you suggest?" he asked mildly.

"Mail them," she said. "I'll reimburse you for the postage." She didn't believe his statement about "business in La Jolla," so if she could convince him to mail the earrings, she'd be safe. Nevertheless, now that he had called her, the eighty-mile barrier that separated them didn't seem so comforting any more.

"Okay," he agreed readily. Too readily.

"I mean it, Bill. I don't want to see you."

His voice rumbled seductively. "Scared, Lila?"

She couldn't answer. Denying it would be an outright lie.

"I miss you, too," he murmured.

"Stop. We can't have this."

"Who says?"

"I do." She pushed herself from the chair and paced the length of the telephone cord. "Do you have a pencil? Here's the address." She dictated rapidly. The earrings were her favorites. She would like them back, if she didn't have to pay too dear a price in terms of her heart.

"Okay. Got it."

"I'm sorry for the extra trouble."

"No trouble, Lila. It's good to hear your voice. I was beginning to wonder if I dreamed last night."

"Bill, we'd better hang up now. Further discussion will only—"

"Of course, if it was a dream, I must have thrashed around a lot," he continued as if she hadn't spoken. "My muscles ache just a bit. A nice ache, though."

"Goodbye, Bill," she said softly. After replacing the receiver, she crossed her arms over her chest and hugged the nervous quivering away. Dammit, he would have to remind her specifically of what they'd shared. She wasn't surprised that he ached. So did she. They'd really made a night of it. And thanks to his call, she was more than ready to do it all again.

She organized some already organized papers on her desk while she composed herself. She couldn't face Tracey in this agitated state. Eventually she became aware that Stevie wasn't crying anymore and Onyx had given up her campaign to get into the office. Turning off the desk lamp, Lila walked to her window and opened the whitewashed shutters. She'd picked this room for herself because it afforded a good view of the water.

The moon wasn't up yet, and the sea was dark as waves rolled toward the beach and La Jolla Cove. She saw a flash of green light and another. Scuba divers were out, as they were almost every night, invisible in their black wetsuits, their green lights dancing like fireflies over the murky surface.

For years Lila had used this view, night or day, as a tranquilizer when life pressed too hard on her. During her divorce she nearly took root here by the window. She had an easy chair beside it, but she didn't sit in the chair now. She and Tracey hadn't eaten supper, and knowing Tracey, nothing would happen in the kitchen until Lila appeared.

She left her office. The voices and music of the television drifted down the hall from the living room, indicating that Tracey had returned to her program. Lila wondered, for the hundredth time, if she ought to assign Tracey the job of making dinner once in a while.

Tracey had fallen easily into the role of child once she'd moved home, and she hadn't taken responsibility for much—except Stevie's care—unless specifically asked. But assigning tasks and creating a routine might subtly suggest that Tracey would be here for an extended stay, and Lila preferred to think of the situation as temporary. Stevie needed his father, inept though the guy seemed to be.

Lila scanned the contents of the refrigerator and pulled out some leftover roast beef and a container of gravy. When the noise of her bustling around didn't bring Tracey from the living room, Lila went to the door of the kitchen. "Tracey? Would you come in and make the salad, please?"

"Sure, Mom." Tracey appeared promptly. She'd never been a reluctant helper, but she wasn't a self-directed one, either. "Who was that on the phone?"

"Someone from the cruise. I accidentally left my earrings on the ship."

"You did?" Tracey began tearing lettuce into a bowl. "Boy, that's one for the books. You never forget anything."

"Well, I did this time."

"Which ones?"

"The antique gold."

Tracey stopped tearing and looked at her mother. "Those expensive ones you and Penny found at a garage sale? I can't believe you'd forget those!"

Lila shrugged. "Maybe my mind's going."

"Like heck. You must have had a wilder time on that cruise than I thought if you misplaced your earrings. Where'd you leave them?"

Lila flushed. "I—well, it really doesn't matter."

Tracey stared, openmouthed. "You're blushing! Was there a man involved in this earring business?"

"Tracey, could we drop it, please?"

"There was! My mother got involved with a man on the cruise and was so distracted she forgot her favorite earrings. I'm stunned. Was that him on the phone?"

"Um, yes."

"And?"

"And nothing." Lila stirred the gravy as if her life depended on it. "He's mailing them back."

"Does he live far?"

"It doesn't matter, Tracey. I'm not seeing him again. Now, if you don't mind, I'd prefer we not discuss the subject again." She mustered her last ounce of maternal authority and glared at her daughter. "Please."

Tracey looked as if someone had awarded her the grand prize in a contest, except that the prize was something she didn't want. Confusion reigned in her eyes as she studied her mother. "Okay, if you insist," she said at last, and returned to her salad making.

They found other subjects with which to fill the silence—Stevie's teething problems, a client of Lila's who was proving difficult, Tracey's latest conclusions about her husband. But toward the end of dinner, Tracey let the conversation lag and withdrew into her own thoughts.

As they were clearing the table, stepping around a hopeful Onyx and Pearl, Tracey spoke. "I know you don't want to talk about this, Mom, but I have to ask one question about this guy from the cruise."

Lila paused, a plate in each hand. "You can ask, but I may choose not to answer."

"I just want to know if you're not seeing him again because you don't want to, or if it has anything to do with me living here."

Lila considered her reply. "I suppose you're part of the reason, Tracey, but there's much more to my decision than your presence here. Once, I didn't want independence, but it was pretty much forced on me. I find that I like being my own boss after all these years and not having someone second-guess all my decisions. I saw this man as a threat to that independence."

"How can you be sure? You must have only known him a little while."

"You'll have to take my word for it, Tracey. So please don't think this is somehow your fault. Encouraging this man would be a mistake for me, whether you were around or not."

"What does Penny say?"

Lila chuckled. "You said only one question. I think that makes three."

"I'll bet Penny's on your case about this. I'm glad she's coming over tomorrow night. She'll tell me what's really going on."

"I'm warning you, if you two start in on me tomorrow night, I'll leave and catch a movie."

Tracey grinned. "We'll be nice. What's his name?"

"Never you mind," Lila said, turning away and carrying the dishes into the kitchen. "The subject's closed."

PENNY ARRIVED the next evening and announced that she'd booked another trip. "I'm touring Navajo Country in Arizona," she told Lila and Tracey as they sat down to dinner. "My travel agent promises there are several single men on this tour." She laughed. "He also suggested I keep my eyes open for a good-looking Navajo."

"Your travel agent knows what you're trying to do?" Tracey asked, wide-eyed.

"Why not?" Penny shrugged. "I almost made him feel guilty enough to give me a refund on the cruise."

"Tell me about the cruise," Tracey said, leaning forward.

Lila glanced up in warning. "Don't fall for that, Penny. I've told Tracey everything she needs to know. I told her that Ensenada was friendly and the ship was luxurious."

Penny's gaze flicked from Lila to Tracey. "I suppose some things are better forgotten."

"Some man called Mom last night about the earrings she left on the ship."

Lila glowered at her daughter.

"Oh, really?" Penny looked delighted. "I didn't realize you'd left your earrings, Lila."

"He's mailing them," Lila said shortly. "Let's eat before the chicken gets cold."

"Mailing them?" Penny protested. "Aw, Lila!"

"He sounded sexy, too," Tracey added with an impish smile.

"Tracey, you're not too big to be sent to your—"

"He is sexy," Penny said, leaning over to Tracey and speaking in a stage whisper. "But I think we'd better cool it or your mother won't invite us back to her dinner table."

Lila cut into her chicken. "You've got that right."

"Tracey, if you want anything interesting to gossip about, you'll have to count on me instead of your mother," Penny said, spooning herself some green beans. "If I had a single thing to report from this cruise, believe me, I would. However, I could have been wearing a nun's habit for all the action I saw. I'm hoping this next trip will be better."

"Are you taking Mom?"

"No, she's not," Lila said, sipping her iced tea. "I'm planning to stay home and mind my own business, literally. The agency doesn't run too well on its own, I've noticed."

"Besides, I discovered that your mom distracts the good-looking ones so much, they're not interested in me," Penny confided.

Tracey lifted her eyebrows and glanced at her mother. "No kidding? You mean she's turning into a fox?"

Lila put down her glass with a force that rattled the ice cubes. "I warned Tracey that I'd take off for the movies if you two got started. I may be able to make the first show," she added, pushing back her chair.

"Wait a minute, Lila." Penny looked contrite. "I'm sorry. We'll talk about something else. So Tracey, what's the latest with what's-his-name?"

"I assume you're referring to the jerk I married."

"That's the one."

Tracey made a face. "Now he claims that this woman in the office started the whole thing. He was an innocent bystander."

Penny stabbed her fork into her salad. "Is that what it looked like to you when you walked in on them?"

"Nope. He looked like a willing participant to me. If I hadn't interrupted when I did, I'm sure they would have gone beyond the kissing stage. You know, with everybody's hands in motion?"

Lila shifted uncomfortably in her seat. That pretty much described the scene Penny had walked in on in their cabin. Lila relaxed when Penny looked at her and winked.

"I know what you mean," Penny said without a trace of antagonism. "So you don't buy the honey-I'm-innocent story. What next?"

"That's up to him," Tracey said. "He's tried about every excuse in the book. He blamed me for being too involved with the baby. Then he said the pressures of work made him vulnerable, now that he's the sole breadwinner. And now he's blaming this woman."

Lila sighed. "Why do men always have to shift the blame? Why can't they just admit that they screwed up and they're sorry?"

"Some can," Penny said. "But you and Tracey seem to attract the other kind." She glanced at Tracey. "Although I have another thought about this current situation of yours."

"Me, too." Tracey laughed. "Like maybe we should string him up by his—"

"Not yet," Penny said. "He's young, Tracey. He's made a mistake."

Tracey narrowed her eyes. "You're not defending him?"

"No. Don't think for a minute I'm taking Mike's side, because I hate what he did. But I wonder if he feels forced to make all these excuses?"

"Who's forcing him?" Tracey asked.

"You."

"Me?" Tracey's mouth dropped open.

"Maybe. By making this such a personal failure that if he admits it, he'd be lower than the low."

"Which he is," Tracey said, eyes glittering.

"Well, it was only a kiss," Penny said.

"But Penny," Lila protested, "what if this is only the beginning of Mike's infidelities? You know how these things get out of hand." Lila spoke in vague terms in front of Tracey, not wanting to bring up her father's transgressions. Penny already knew the whole sordid story.

"Yes, I know." Penny gave Lila an understanding look. "Forget what I said. Mike is probably a rat and deserves whatever punishment he gets." She took a sip of tea. "Have you guys heard about Canyon de Chelly?"

"I think so," Lila said, grateful to Penny for switching topics.

"That's one of the stops on my Navajo Country tour," Penny continued, "and it's supposed to be spectacular. They have this one spire that rises eight hundred feet from the canyon floor, and it's not as big around as this house. Can you imagine?"

"Nope," Tracey said, her face relaxing into a smile. "Sounds like a huge phallic symbol to me."

Lila choked on her green beans. "I didn't think you knew that word."

"Which one?" Tracey asked with a mischievous grin. "Come on, Mom. I've been to college and I'm married.

You ought to loosen up around me. I'm not a kid anymore. Neither's Sarah."

"I suppose not," Lila said. "Still, it comes as a shock the first time you hear your daughter calmly discussing phallic symbols in public."

"Actually I agree with you, Tracey," Penny said. "I hope the rock will, if you pardon the pun, 'in-spire' the men on this trip."

Tracey and Lila groaned together.

"I thought it was rather clever," Penny said with a sniff. "But some people just can't appreciate wittiness, I guess. And speaking of Sarah, any word on her studies?"

"I'm afraid so," Lila said. "A letter arrived today from the dean. Sarah's not 'applying herself,' as the phrase goes."

Penny frowned. "That's too bad. I wonder if—" She paused as the doorbell chimed. "Were you expecting someone?"

"No." Lila got up. "Jackie down the street said she'd be by some time to collect for the cancer drive. It's probably her. I'll be right back."

As she walked through the living room to the entry hall, Lila considered what Penny had said about Mike and Tracey. Maybe Penny was right, and the incident with the co-worker in Mike's office had been blown out of proportion. Lila realized that her own bad experience with Stan might be coloring her judgment. As for Tracey, she probably suspected far more than Lila had told her about the problems that drove her mother and father apart. She might be overreacting as a result of having the same fear—that Mike would become a philanderer like her father. On the other hand, Lila didn't know that Mike *wouldn't* turn out that way, either.

Still mulling over the problem, she opened the door.

"Your earrings."

She blinked and stared. "B—Bill?"

"So shoot me. I couldn't mail them."

Her first impulse was to hurl herself into his arms; her second rational one was to take the earrings and say goodbye. Before she could do either, Penny's greeting ended the inner debate.

"Bill Windsor?" Penny, followed by Tracey, bustled through the living room to stand beside Lila. "I thought I heard that sexy baritone! Bill, I want you to meet Lila's daughter, Tracey."

Lila glanced across at Tracey, curious as a kitten, giving Bill the once-over. Lila tried to figure out how she could gracefully end the tableau and close the door with Bill still on the other side of it. Finally, she gave up and invited him in.

"Have some dessert with us, Bill," Penny said, taking his arm and ignoring Lila's glare. "We just finished dinner, but if you're hungry, we could rustle up some leftover—"

"I'm fine, Penny, thanks. Dessert would be nice, though."

"And coffee," Penny added. "Tracey, you and I can make coffee and cut the cherry pie while these two visit."

"Okay." Tracey allowed herself to be led away, although she kept glancing back at her mother and Bill. Penny got her inside the kitchen and flipped the swinging louvered door closed, blocking them from sight if not from sound.

Lila heard their muffled giggles once the door was closed. She considered marching in there and giving them a piece of her mind, except that Bill would hear everything through the louvers. "Let's go into the living room," she suggested, figuring she'd work out some measure of privacy for what she had to say to him.

"Sure." Bill followed her into the room.

"Bill," she began, turning to face him. "You can't—"

"This is quite a house." His glance took in the white marble fireplace, the framed seascapes, the beamed ceilings.

"We got a good price, years ago," Lila said. "Being in the real estate business helps. Listen, before they arrive with the dessert, why don't you just—"

"I'm not surprised your home looks like this. Is that vase crystal?"

"Yes, but I got it at a garage sale. Bill, I don't want to be rude, but you're forcing me to be. You'll have to leave."

He studied her, a smile on his face. "Good."

"Excuse me?"

"You're upset. That's good. I told myself if you handled me like any other uninvited guest, I'd be wasting my time. But my being here agitates you. That means you haven't been able to put the other night behind you, either."

"I'm working on that," she said, keeping her voice low, "and your presence here doesn't help. I'd appreciate it if you'd go quietly out the front door. I'll explain to Tracey and Penny that you remembered another engagement."

He stepped closer, surrounding her with the scent of his recent shower and shave. He hadn't come here looking like a garage mechanic. He'd worn a tie and sportcoat, as he had on the cruise. "But I have a weakness for cherry pie," he said softly.

"You can get that anywhere." Her heart clamored in her chest.

"That's true." His voice grew silky. "But quality is hard to find."

"Don't you dare touch me," she whispered.

"I don't have to."

She clenched her hands in front of her to still the trembling that threatened to prove him right. "Just go," she begged. Behind her the kitchen door squeaked. Too late. Tracey and Penny were arriving with dessert.

"Here we are," Penny announced, bearing a tray of pie plates while Tracey followed with mugs and a carafe of coffee. "We nuked the pie and slapped on ice cream. I hope that's how you like it, Bill."

"Just right," Bill said, lowering himself into one of four white upholstered chairs that surrounded a polished walnut coffee table. He accepted a plate from Penny. "Thanks. Looks great. I was complimenting Lila on this room, although it beats me how she manages to keep it like this with a baby around."

"He hasn't been able to reach anything yet," Tracey said, moving the crystal vase to make room for the coffee and mugs on the table. "But he's starting to pull himself up, so it won't be long before stuff like this'll have to go."

"Oh, I don't know," Lila said, vaguely irritated at Tracey's decorating presumptions. "We could teach him not to touch certain things." She took her plate from Penny without returning Penny's smile. She'd deal with her best friend later.

Tracey laughed as she poured the coffee and passed it around. "Maybe you want to keep track of Stevie every minute, Mom, but I don't. I think we'd better put the breakables away."

"We'll see. We still have time to decide." Lila's irritation grew and finally she realized the cause. She was seeing this situation as Bill might see it. During the cruise, he'd called Tracey's presence here an imposition, and with all this talk of sweeping the room clean of crystal, baskets of shells, flower arrangements, books—in essence, all the charm she'd worked so hard to create—she felt imposed upon for the first time.

"Terrific pie," Bill said, slicing off another chunk with his fork.

"That's Penny's contribution," Lila said quickly. "I seldom bake."

"That's for sure," Tracey added. "When we were little, she made cookies and stuff all the time, but now I have to depend on Penny."

Lila was shocked at the immaturity revealed by Tracey's statement. Somewhere along the line Tracey had missed the idea that at twenty-four, with a child and a husband, she'd better depend upon herself, and for more than cookies. She'd have a serious talk with Tracey very soon.

"More pie, Bill?" Penny asked.

"No, but that was great." He set down his plate and settled back in his chair with his coffee mug. He crossed his ankle over his knee and loosened his tie, not the actions of a man who intended to leave soon, Lila thought. "So where is this little guy you bought the chair for?" he asked, turning toward Lila.

"He's asleep," she replied.

Bill pushed back his sleeve to look at his watch. "Guess it is a little late for babies to be up."

Penny set down her cup as if a sudden inspiration had struck her. "Tracey! We could still make the eight o'clock showing of that movie we wanted to see."

Tracey popped up on cue. "You're right! Oh, Mom, Penny and I have been dying to see this, and you don't care about horror flicks."

"That's for sure," Lila said, smelling a conspiracy.

"Would you sit for Stevie so we can go?" Tracey asked, all innocence and blinking blue eyes.

"I hope you won't think us rude, Bill." Penny left her chair and gathered up the empty plates. "But I think this is the last night for this movie."

Lila didn't believe that for one minute. Obviously, they were hoping to leave her alone with Bill.

"No problem," Bill said. "Lila and I can take care of the dishes."

Lila's jaw dropped. What gall! But she recovered herself enough to smile sweetly. "That won't be necessary. In fact, I work much faster alone, and I have some paperwork to catch up on after those days out of the office. These two are off to the movies, and I know you must be anxious to get back on the road."

Penny looked worried that her plan might fizzle. "At any rate, Tracey and I do have to run. Get your coat, Tracey. I'll treat."

"Bill's probably blocking you in the driveway," Lila said, rising from her chair. "He could leave first."

"Actually I'm not blocking anyone," Bill said, remaining where he was. "I noticed the car parked there and left mine in the street."

"How thoughtful," Penny said, pulling on her coat. "Well, we're off. Nice seeing you again, Bill."

"Yes, nice meeting you, Mr. Windsor," Tracey added.

The two scurried out the door amid more muffled giggles, and Lila turned to find Bill on his feet and moving toward her. They were alone, with nothing between them but her resolve.

9

BILL NOTICED THE LINES of tension bracketing Lila's eyes and mouth. This wasn't the carefree woman who had come to him in his cabin. Yet even in her navy business dress, with her conservative strand of pearls and her hair pulled back in a no-nonsense clip at the nape of her neck, she moved him as no woman had in years. Maybe ever.

"Don't think that because they're gone you can—"

"Lila." He dared to grasp her arms and his fingers absorbed her slight shiver. "I thought when you were out of the picture I'd be able to accept our decision of never seeing each other again. Instead, I've been going slowly crazy. When I saw you standing in the doorway tonight, my head cleared for the first time in two days."

Her chin lifted. She was obviously still trying to resist the pull of this powerful attraction. "Nothing's changed since we said goodbye. As you see, my daughter and grandson are still here and I'm not about to start anything that would create an awkward situation."

"We can work around them." He eased her nearer, held his breath. At any moment she could fling herself away from him and he'd have to start all over, waste precious time.

"I don't care to do that."

He watched her lips part, her pupils widen as desire unfolded within her. He gripped her arms and snugged her in tight. "I think you do," he said, bending toward the lips that beckoned, no matter what words came out of them. "I may not have learned everything about you in that cabin, but I know when you want me."

She whimpered and put her hands on his shoulders as if to push him away. He didn't give her the chance. He put everything he had into the kiss, and gradually her arms slid around his neck and she arched her body in the way he remembered, the way he might never forget. He held her against his throbbing groin and felt the heat in her, too. His memory filled in the delicious moistness waiting for him and he groaned with impatience. He lifted his mouth from hers. "Your bedroom. Where is it?"

"We can't, Bill." Her voice was shaky.

"Yes, we can. They won't be back for more than an hour."

"But they'll know."

"I don't care."

"I do," she said, still sounding unconvinced.

"More than this?" He cupped her behind and pushed against her. Her eyes closed. He rubbed the small of her back and moved his hips—teasing, tempting. She grew warmer, more pliable.

Finally, a soft murmuring breath escaped her lips. "Down the hall," she whispered, and opened her eyes. "I must be insane. Trying to grab a quick—"

He silenced her with a light touch of his finger. "That's not what this is about at all. And an hour's not that quick."

"You'll have to be gone before then."

He would have liked to complain about a forty-five-year-old woman whose sex life was determined by what her married daughter would think, but he decided that wouldn't be in his best interests at the moment.

As he followed her down the dim hallway he tripped over something furry. Both he and the furry thing yowled. "What the hell was that?" he cried, regaining his balance.

"Onyx, my cat," she replied, just as Stevie started to wail. "And that's the baby," she added with a sigh and released his hand.

"Can't you shove one of those rubber doodads in his mouth?"

"Tracey doesn't believe in pacifiers. I'll have to rock him."

Bill searched his long-ago experiences with babies for an alternative to losing contact with Lila at this crucial moment. "Maybe if we're real quiet he'll go back to sleep."

She ignored his suggestion and opened the door to the room where the wailing was coming from. He followed, not having much choice. The room smelled the way Jason's had when he was little—sweet and powdery. Moonlight shone through the gauzy curtains at the window and picked up Lila's silhouette as she held the baby and crooned softly.

Bill could tell right away she loved the little kid. She wasn't acting impatient and resentful in the least. Her daughter had a good deal with a grandma like this. Too good a deal, unfortunately, Bill thought. Tracey and her baby were interfering with what could be a beautiful series of evenings for him and this passionate woman.

He calculated how much momentum they'd lost by waking up the baby just now. Ever since starting out on this trip he'd wondered if it would be a total waste of time. Now he pretty much guessed it was. Walking around with the baby would give Lila time to reconsider, and when Stevie was asleep, she'd ask Bill to leave—again. And he would. A guy's ego could be expected to take only so much.

Stevie's crying ebbed into occasional snuffles. Lila eased him back into the crib and leaned over the rail to stroke his back. Bill ached just watching her. Babies got stroked by crying. Men weren't allowed that tactic.

At last she straightened up and motioned to him that they could leave the room. More alert to the possibility of a cat underfoot, he watched the floor as he moved ahead of her into the hall. Apparently the cat—he couldn't remember what she'd called it, something like 'obnoxious'—wasn't around to trip him up this time. Naturally. Now it didn't matter.

As Lila quietly closed Stevie's door, Bill braced himself for rejection. He was half-turned toward the living room when she took his hand and tugged gently in the other direction. He couldn't believe it, but neither did he question it. What he did do was watch for cats.

Her room was at the end of the hall and faced the water, if he had his directions straight. He couldn't be positive because louvered shutters covered the tall windows and subdued the pounding surf to a whisper. He noticed an exterior door that probably led to a balcony, streamlined walnut furniture contrasting with white walls, and a king-size platform bed covered with a cream-colored comforter. In the middle of the bed, nearly camouflaged, was a cream-colored cat.

"This is Pearl," Lila said, picking up the cat and holding her close for Bill's inspection.

"Hello, Pearl." He didn't think this was the time to tell her he detested cats. Pearl hissed and swiped at his face with claws extended. Bill drew back just in time to save himself from having his face ripped. "Nice cat."

"Pearl!" Lila scolded. "Bad kitty! Just for that you have to leave the room."

Bill lifted his gaze heavenward. Someone was watching out for him tonight, no doubt about it. He'd never made love to a woman while a cat was present, and he didn't relish the idea. Cats, he knew, pounced on moving objects. And cats had claws.

Lila set Pearl outside the door and closed it. Then she turned and leaned against the door, a seductive smile curving her lips. "Ready for a meeting of SPOT?"

"You haven't forgotten." He dispensed with his coat and pulled off his tie as he crossed the room.

"Sexual Pleasure Organization for Two? How could I forget?"

"I thought once that baby cried, we were finished."

She snuggled into his embrace. "That's because you don't know everything about me."

"I'm ready to learn." He kissed her forehead and savored the flutter of her fingers unfastening the buttons of his shirt. He still couldn't quite believe that he would be making love to her again. But he hadn't been able to accept not doing so, either.

"I realized something when I was holding Stevie," she said, pulling his shirt open and kissing his skin. "I realized how cuddling that little baby makes me so grateful to be alive. And in an entirely different way,

I've experienced that vivid connection to life, that gratitude, one other time."

"I hope I can guess when it was."

She gazed up at him, her expression open and giving, just as he'd remembered. "You can. And I want to feel that way again."

"So do I, sweet lady," he murmured, unsnapping the clip from her hair. "So do I."

She stood on tiptoe and nibbled at his lower lip. "Indulge me," she whispered.

He thought his heart would pound right out of his chest. "Anything," he said, his voice more husky than he was used to.

"Carry me to the bed. Undress me. I know we haven't much time, but—"

He picked her up before she could finish. He loved the feeling of mastery the action gave him and wondered why he'd never tried it before. He settled her on the cream-colored comforter and began uncovering the wonders of her body. Her skin blushed for him wherever he touched, kissed, teased, until she was rosy and warm, damp and sighing with pleasure.

He stood and gazed down at his handiwork. Her eyes were wide and dark with longing, her lips swollen from kissing. She breathed in quick, shallow gasps that made her breasts and her peaked ready nipples quiver. Lower, her hips moved restlessly, calling attention to the moist dark triangle and her creamy thighs, dew-sprinkled, inviting....

He discarded his clothes but remembered the small package he'd tucked into his pants pocket, wondering at the time if he would use it. He tore it open now. When he was finished he glanced up and found her watching him, her expression hungry. No words were needed. She spread her thighs and he moved between them, coming home.

He pushed in deep and groaned with satisfaction. Her grip on his buttocks told him she wanted all he could give her, so he drew back gently and shoved forward once again. He was rewarded with her gasp of affirmation. He clenched his teeth against the surge that threatened to end this long-awaited coupling and began the rhythm that they'd worked out, in exquisite detail, through the long night they'd spent together.

He felt her response build quickly to match his own. Neither of them would last long, he knew, but he tried to draw out the pleasure nevertheless. Finally, she begged him for release, and with mingled cries they tilted over the edge of restraint.

BY THE TIME Tracey and Penny returned from the movies, Bill was gone and Lila was dressed and going through the motions of working in her study. Both cats were curled up under the desk at her feet and she had tuned in a classical music station on the radio. She gave every appearance of being engrossed in her papers, although she hadn't accomplished anything since she sat down. Therefore, she could hardly object when Penny and Tracey boiled into her study without apology and immediately pounced on the subject of Bill.

"If you got rid of him and have been in here all evening working, I'll never forgive you," Penny announced.

"Yeah, Mom. Don't tell us we went to the movies for nothing, because it wasn't even that good. So what happened? He is pretty cute, by the way, for an old guy."

Lila gazed at them. "I'm not going to tell you what happened," she said.

Penny whooped. "That's a good sign, Trace! A very good sign."

"So, Mom, is he coming back? Penny says he lives in Mission Viejo. Will he be driving down other times?"

"I doubt it," Lila said.

Penny's elation faded. "Why not? Why the heck not? The guy's nuts about you, and I saw the way you looked at him. Why aren't you seeing him again?"

"I didn't say I wasn't seeing him again. He has a race on Saturday, and I'm driving up for it."

"Hey, that's great!" Penny said.

Lila glanced at her. "Guess I won't be able to go garage saling with you that day, after all."

"Don't give that another thought. We can 'sail' those old garages any time. This is far more important, although I'm surprised at the activity. I didn't think you cared for car racing."

Lila blushed. "Well, I don't, but—"

"But that doesn't matter," Penny finished, throwing both arms in the air. "You just want to be with him. Lila, I'm so happy for you."

"Gosh," Tracey mused, peering at Lila. "I can't quite take it in. My mother has a boyfriend."

Lila frowned. "I don't know if I'd call him that."

"We won't call him anything, honey," Penny said, patting Lila's cheek. "He's all yours, to name and enjoy. Will you be staying up there through the weekend?"

"I . . . I'd planned on it."

Tracey stared. "Overnight?"

Lila avoided her gaze. "Well—yes."

"Tracey, put your eyes back in your head," Penny said. "Your mother is certainly entitled to make those kinds of plans if she wishes. I think she's old enough and wise enough to have a lover, don't you?"

"S-sure," Tracey stammered, "but you just never think of your own mother as—"

"Then don't think about it," Penny advised. "But don't you dare put a crimp in her style, or I'll paddle your behind, even if you are twenty-four years old."

"Well, I wasn't . . . I mean, I wouldn't."

Lila recovered her poise enough to step in. "I'm not exactly comfortable with this, either, Tracey. It's not as if I've been totally celibate since the divorce, but I never let you girls know before if I . . . became intimate with someone."

This new revelation toppled Tracey into a nearby armchair. "This has happened before?"

"Well, sort of. Not much, and I never stayed the night with anyone."

"Who were they?"

Penny gave Tracey a reproving glance. "You don't have to know who."

"I hope not any of those geeks you dated, Mom. I hope it was at least with someone halfway decent, like Bill."

Lila gazed at her daughter with a half smile. "You approve of Bill, then?"

"I guess. So far."

"And I definitely approve," Penny added. "Now if I could only find someone that yummy for myself, my world would be complete."

Lila gazed at her friend with love. Penny was a terrific loser. "Someone will come along," she said. "You're too good a woman to be lonely much longer."

Tracey chuckled. "If you don't find someone soon, your travel agent will be a wealthy man."

"Yeah, well, at least I'm making one guy happy," Penny said, reaching over to muss Tracey's hair. "Come on, let's finish the rest of that cherry pie before I go home."

The three of them sat at the kitchen table drinking decaf coffee and polishing off the rest of the pie while they joked about how many hours of aerobics they'd have to do in penance for two pieces of pie in one night. Finally, Tracey convinced Penny that the two of them wouldn't have to work out, because neither of them were worried about impressing a man at the moment. Lila, on the other hand, would be wise to cut out treats, they added, giggling as she blushed bright red.

Eventually Penny left, but Tracey seemed unwilling to go to bed. She helped Lila load the dessert plates into the dishwasher and described the plot of the movie she and Penny had seen. Lila felt that Tracey had something on her mind, but Lila waited, less sure of herself around Tracey than she had been before tonight.

"Mom," Tracey said at last, folding and unfolding the kitchen towel. "I think I'm in the way here."

"Nonsense," Lila said immediately, reflexively. "We've been through that. I love having you and Stevie around."

"I know, but when I asked you before about this guy, you said there were lots of reasons you didn't want to keep seeing him. Except now you *are* seeing him, but you have to drive up there to do it, so you can be alone, I guess. I think I'm the only problem."

Lila sank into a kitchen chair and Onyx jumped into her lap. "Look, you and I are new at this," she said, stroking the cat's ebony fur, "and I won't deny that I'd feel uncomfortable having him spend the weekend here."

"See? That only proves that—"

"But," Lila interrupted, holding up one hand, "not just because you're here. I'm not sure I'm ready for a man to invade what's become my space. Since your dad and I divorced, I've become more territorial."

Tracey grinned. "Like a cat."

"And that's another thing. I don't think he likes cats."

"So? Neither did Dad, but we still had cats."

"I know." Lila sighed. "It isn't just that, it's everything." She looked at her daughter. "Men take up space. Lots of space."

Tracey nodded. "I know. Sometimes Mike's and my apartment seemed so small."

"Speaking of Mike, have you thought at all about what Penny said?"

"What do you mean?"

"That maybe what he did was blown a little out of proportion?"

"Mom! What he did was *unforgivable*." She narrowed her eyes. "Or is it that you want me to make up with him so I'll go back? I still think—"

"Tracey, bag it. I'm not trying to force you out. Believe me."

"That's good, because I don't know if I can ever go back to him, Mom. If I'm in the way, I'll find somewhere else to go. I'm not sure where, but I'm sure someone could take me in."

Lila groaned. Tracey was feeling sorry for herself. It might even be partly because her love life was in a shambles, while her mother seemed to be starting out on a new adventure of the heart. Lila had overcome Penny's jealousy only to have to deal with her daughter's. "You're not moving out, Tracey, and that's that," she said, getting up to hug her daughter.

"Thanks, Mom," Tracey said, hugging back with more force than usual. "Let's go to bed. It's been a long night."

"Yes, it has." Lila turned on the dishwasher and flipped off the kitchen light after Tracey left. Lila had the vague feeling that she'd come out on the short end of her exchange with Tracey. Somehow Tracey had put her into the position of insisting that her daughter stay in the house; yet recently, even before Bill had become a consideration, Lila had been wondering if the arrangement was to everyone's benefit, especially her own. Although she enjoyed being a grandmother, she was beginning to tire of the role of mother. Tracey's presence seemed to keep her locked into that role, whether she liked it or not.

LILA HAD AGREED to meet Bill at the track and follow him home after the race. He had implied that if they met at his house, they might never get to the track, and he had an obligation to his pit crew.

On Saturday morning Lila chose the efficiency of the interstate over the charm of the Coast road. She'd never liked driving on freeways, despite a lifetime of dealing with them, but she couldn't ask for better conditions than she had that morning. Traffic was no worse than usual and the fall day was clear. Trees on the hillsides responded to the season with a faint show of color. Lila switched on the radio and tried to convince herself that the drive wasn't so bad.

Yet, as the road curved inevitably inland, away from the endless horizon of the Pacific, she felt the familiar loss of something important. She wished that Bill lived, as she did, by the water. She had to assume he'd chosen not to, while she had made it one of her cherished goals. Part of her original interest in real estate had stemmed from her passion to live by the water and the bargain hunting that would entail. She and Stan had indeed found a bargain, one she could never afford at current prices. She often marveled at the escalating value of her house, but it didn't matter, because she had no intention of selling.

She took the exit Bill had indicated and found the track with no trouble. The sound of whining engines sent out a signal from several blocks away. Lila shook her head. Never in her wildest dreams had she pictured herself in an environment like this.

She parked in the dirt lot flanking the banner-draped grandstands and walked past booths selling everything from chili dogs to racing caps. Fine dust settled over her jeans and short-sleeved blue sweater, and she was glad that she'd worn a simple outfit. Penny, who'd actually been to a race before, had guided her on that decision.

Bill had left instructions at the gate, and when Lila gave her name, a buxom young woman in a Penzoil cap fastened a plastic strip around Lila's wrist. "That'll get you into the pit," she said.

Lila bought a program and entered the grandstand area. She wasn't sure the pit was where she belonged, but Bill had insisted. By now the noise was deafening. He'd told her that he wouldn't run until the fourth race, so she had timed her arrival for the third one, mentioning that she wasn't keen on loud noise. Bill had promised that she'd get used to the noise. Lila wondered when.

Trying to get the lay of the land, she stood out of the way of spectators who seemed to know where they were headed. She figured out that the noise was worst here, at the grandstands, because that was one of two straightaways on the oval track, and the drivers always sped up on the straightaways. The scream of engines going full-out bounced off the metal grandstands, increasing the racket.

The cars circling the track weren't what she'd expected. Volkswagens, Datsuns and Hondas not too different from the ones with which she'd shared the freeway battled each other at the turns, sometimes bumping fenders. Yet, as she looked more closely, she could tell the cars were different from street vehicles. For one thing, they were decorated with large numbers and stickers advertising various motor products. They also had some sort of thick support rods inside, probably in case they rolled or crashed, Lila decided. The driver's window was a net instead of glass, no doubt for the same reason.

Rolled or crashed. She hadn't allowed that aspect to surface in her mind until now. Bill would soon drive one of those cars with the extra supports and the net window. She recalled a conversation on the ship, in which Penny had talked about Bill's daredevil behavior, and his son's concern. Penny's job would have been to settle Bill down. Lila had scoffed at the idea of such manipulation, but that was before she'd learned to care for him, learned—she might as well face it—to love him.

Amidst the grit and clamor, gas fumes and screams of the crowd, Lila finally admitted to herself that she loved Bill Windsor. He'd called her every night after his unexpected visit. She'd learned more about his job and the reasons he enjoyed it. She'd discussed her agency— but more important, she'd told him the story of her divorce. His sympathetic response did more to build her trust than anything they'd shared thus far. Without actually saying so, Bill had convinced her that she could count on his honesty.

Lila's reluctance to venture into the alien world of race cars disappeared in the face of a more urgent need to see Bill. She touched the arm of a man passing by with a paper cup full of beer. "Where's the pit?" she yelled over the engine noise.

"Across the track!" he yelled back. "You'll have to wait until this race is over, and then they'll let you through!"

"Thanks!" She looked over at the area he'd indicated, in the middle of the oval. Before, she'd seen only an undifferentiated mass of people and cars. Now that she knew Bill was there, she squinted to catch a glimpse of him. He'd told her his car was Number Nine, a Corvette, but she couldn't find it in the jumble of people, trailers, and other race cars.

She opened her program and scanned it. Sure enough, he was listed in the fourth race and the number of the car was nine. The program notes included a description of the race as a "monster event" featuring the heaviest cars with the biggest engines. The description did nothing to calm her fears. She also found pictures of the drivers, and there was Bill, grinning into the camera, his hair mussed from the helmet he held on one hip, his one-piece racing suit unzipped to his waist and a wet-looking T-shirt underneath.

The other drivers pictured in the program, who ranged in age from nineteen to sixty and included one woman, all wore the same crazy grin. Lila noticed biographical information that listed occupations of dentistry, law, and college teaching. This amateur racing, Lila concluded, was a Walter Mitty dream come true for these people. She hoped that she wouldn't ruin everything by being petrified of the risk Bill was taking.

At last, the checkered flag waved over the first car, and the race drew to a close. When the last car crossed the finish line, Lila joined others gathering at the gate to be ushered across to the pit. She hoped she could locate Bill before his race started. Not that she planned to do anything dramatic, like making a declaration of love. She just wanted to see him, to touch his hand, to see his smile for real and not in a black-and-white photo. She might never tell him she was in love with him. So much about their relationship was a shifting mosaic of possibilities, and speaking of love might freeze them both into uncomfortable positions.

As she started across the track, which was hot from the sun and the friction of rubber, she saw him on the other side, waiting for her. His jumpsuit hung at his waist, and his T-shirt looked damp, just as it had in the picture. His grin was the same, too. She waved and quickened her pace. Before she realized it, she was practically running, and when he scooped her into his arms, she kissed him without considering who might be watching.

"You're here," he said, holding her tightly and gazing into her face.

The joy of being with him overwhelmed her and she nearly blurted out her feelings. Yet she knew that could be an irreparable mistake. "Yes, I'm here," she said.

10

"COME ON," Bill said, his arm around Lila's shoulders as he propelled her through the crowd. "I want you to meet my pit crew."

"Is Jason one of them?"

"No. Jason disapproves of this, but even if he didn't, he couldn't help, anyway. He left for Boston this week." He glanced down at her. "You'll have to tolerate being alone in the house with me."

"Could be tough." She slid her arm around his waist over the bulky suit and gave him a squeeze. Being near him again made her light-headed with desire, and the strangeness of their surroundings encouraged her to cling to him as if he were an anchor.

"Damn, but you look good to me," he murmured. "Something tells me I'll finish this race in record time, just so I can get back to you."

"Bill, don't do anything—" she caught herself in time "—I wouldn't do," she finished, avoiding the warning, a Penny type of warning, that had almost popped out.

"From the look on your face when you crossed that track, you'd also drive like a maniac to get this race out of the way, if our places were switched."

"I was a little bit glad to see you," she said.

"Then I can hardly wait until you're overjoyed." He pointed to an egg-yolk colored Corvette with a large black number nine painted on the side and two men working under the hood. "There's the car."

"Wow." The Corvette reminded her of a crouched leopard—fast and dangerous. "Looks powerful," she said, concealing her anxiety as best she could. Lila wanted this relationship to be based on freedom, not dependence and fear. If Bill wanted to race cars, she'd swallow the temptation to caution him.

"It's fun to drive," he said. "Maybe sometime you—"

"Oh, I don't think so, Bill," she said quickly.

"That's right. You're the woman who plays nickel slots one nickel at a time," he teased. He guided her around to the front of the car. "Jack, Raphael, I'd like you to meet Lila Kedge. Lila, Jack's the handsome blond devil and Raphael's our resident Latin lover."

Both men laughed.

"Don't let him kid you," Raphael said, wiping his hand on a rag before offering to shake hands with Lila. "We agreed to be his pit crew because he promised that racing brings fame and gorgeous women. He neglected to mention that all that goes to the driver, not the pit crew."

"Ain't that the truth," Jack said, glancing up from his work. "Excuse my manners, Lila, but I'm heavily involved with this carburetor and can't shake hands." He glanced at Raphael. "Could that be the reason we can't get women? That we smell of grease and exhaust fumes and have shirts decorated with oil stains, while glamour-boy here just has to sit behind the wheel and steer?"

"That must be it," Bill said, chuckling, "because you boys are as charming as the day is long. In fact, I picked you for your charm."

"The hell you did," Raphael said. "Whoops, sorry Lila."

"Raphael," Jack asked in a falsetto, "could you take your charming self and step on the gas, so I can listen to this thing when it's revved up a tad?"

"Delighted," Raphael said. He sat in the driver's seat and gunned the motor until Lila thought her eardrums would break. Then he let it idle again. "How's that, Jack, sweetie?"

"Lovely."

Raphael came back to stand beside Lila. "You seem like a sensible woman. Can't imagine what you're doing with Billy-goat Windsor here," he said, grinning. "He's probably got you fooled into thinking he's some hot-shot driver."

Lila smiled at the nickname.

"I am a hotshot driver," Bill said, peering under the hood.

"Win this race and prove it," Jack said, twisting a screw on the carburetor.

"Tune that thing right and I will."

"Billy-goat, this baby is always tuned right."

The announcer called for the cars in race four, and Bill slipped his arms into the sleeves of his suit. "They're playing our tune," he said, zipping up the suit.

"Let's hope you dance like an angel," Jack said, slamming the hood closed. "I've done all I can."

Raphael handed Bill his helmet and driving gloves. "Watch out for that guy from Nevada," he said. "He's supposed to be murder on the turns."

"And listen to the engine," Jack added. "We don't want to blow another one."

"I always listen," Bill said, "except when I'm about to crash into a wall. That distracts me somehow."

"Don't see why," Jack said, smiling. "Wouldn't bother me. I'd still listen."

"That's why I'm driving and you're in the pit," Bill said, clapping him on the arm. Then he turned to Lila. "This is it. Give me some luck."

She kissed him quickly on the cheek.

He raised one eyebrow. "That wouldn't take me around the first turn," he said, grabbing her for a full-blown kiss that left her blushing. "Let's do it!" He pulled up his knit face protector and strapped on his helmet, disguising the man Lila knew, leaving in his place someone mysterious and intimidating.

She stepped back as he climbed behind the wheel and his two-man crew pushed the car into its starting position. She noticed other women following their men out on the track, but she wasn't ready for that kind of involvement in this sport. Besides, Jack and Raphael were still giving last-minute advice and instructions, and she had nothing to contribute, especially after Bill's searing kiss had left her mush-brained.

The signal came to start the engines and the roar assaulted her ears. The pit had been aptly named, she decided. She felt at the bottom of one, surrounded by growling monsters. The man sitting in car number nine seemed totally unrelated to the one who had made love to her a week ago. She hoped that this feeling of detachment would last and soften her anxiety as the cars careened around the track.

No such luck. The moment he pulled away for the pace lap, her stomach twisted with fear. She'd never been good at watching her loved ones take risks. As

Tracey and Sarah had progressed through riding bikes in traffic, to driving and learning to water-ski, Lila's imagination had manufactured grisly pictures of broken bones and bashed heads.

"He'll be all right," Raphael said, coming to stand beside her.

"I—I'm sure he will," she managed.

"Although I'm afraid your program's unreadable by now," he added.

She glanced down at the mangled tube of paper that she clutched in a death grip. "Maybe I am a bit nervous," she admitted with a small smile.

"Does Bill know that this scares you?"

Lila shook her head.

Raphael stuck his hands into his jeans pockets and looked toward the far turn as the engine noise increased a notch. "Does it scare you enough that you'd want him to quit?" he asked casually.

"Yes," she said, and watched Raphael's head snap around toward her. "But I would never ask him not to race," she added, and his frown disappeared.

"That's good. I've known women who were on guys all the time about the danger. It poisoned the relationship."

"I can imagine it would."

The announcer kept up a steady patter announcing the cars as they cruised toward the starting line. His voice grew more enthusiastic, and finally he shouted "They're off!"

The cars leaped ahead, unleashed from their prescribed positions, and a black Corvette swerved dangerously close to Bill's fender. Lila gasped.

"You don't have to watch," Raphael counseled. "We have some lawn chairs you can sit in, and a newspaper to read, and even a cold beer to drink."

She looked up at him. "Thanks, but no thanks. As long as I can hear it, I couldn't block it out."

"He's leading!" Jack ran toward them from the infield where he'd been watching the far side of the track. "He beat that bastard on the last turn!" He glanced at Lila. "Uh, I mean—"

"Look, both of you, forget I'm here. I'm forty-five years old and I've certainly heard about all the swear words that exist," Lila said. "Oh, no, here they come." She stared down the track at the close-knit pack, with the yellow Corvette leading by a small margin. The black car growled at his rear fender, inches away.

The engines screamed through the straightaway as the excited announcer shouted the order of cars with Bill Windsor in car number nine leading. Lila was astonished to discover a thrill of pride mixed in with her terror.

"Go, Billy-goat!" Raphael and Jack yelled together as he passed.

Lila couldn't cheer. But she hoped he'd stay in front. That seemed to be the best place to keep from crashing. But when the cars whizzed by again, she was denied even that comfort. The black car led, with Bill a close second. Raphael and Jack screamed themselves hoarse and waved their arms in the air. Lila twisted her program until it shredded in half.

She counted every lap. Her throat was dry, every muscle in her body tense. Bill and the black car traded places, then traded again as tires screeched in the turns and Lila pictured impending collisions and twisted metal. Through the ordeal she heard enough of the announcer's patter to realize that the black car was the one from Nevada, the one Raphael had warned Bill about, the one who was murder on the turns. Lila prayed.

"This is it!" Jack crowed. "And I know he's gonna do it."

Bill was proclaimed in the lead going into the final turn, and Lila crossed her fingers and closed her eyes as tires squealed. At the sound of the crash, her eyes flew open and her skin grew cold as ice. Both Raphael and Jack started running toward the noise and she followed, forcing her legs to carry her through the obstacle course of people and equipment as the announcer explained that the two lead cars had collided on the turn.

"It's okay!" Jack called over his shoulder as the announcer said basically the same thing. "Here he comes!"

Lila nearly ran into Raphael, and they both stared as the yellow Corvette roared toward them, a dent in the right rear fender. The black car followed, but had no chance as Bill barreled toward the finish line. The black-and-white checkered flag waved him through and he stuck one gloved hand out the window in salute. The announcer proclaimed that Bill Windsor would now take his victory lap.

Jack and Raphael went crazy hugging each other and Lila. As soon as they stopped hugging her and she had no physical support, she sat right down on the ground. The men didn't notice what had happened to her at first, as others came up to congratulate them.

Eventually, Raphael looked for her and spied her sitting on the ground. "You okay?" he asked, peering down at her.

"I'm exhausted," she replied truthfully. "I couldn't stand up anymore."

"Here." Raphael helped her up. "Lean on me. You did real good, but I have a piece of advice for you. Bill would kill me for saying this, but I don't think you should come to these."

"But racing is so important to him," Lila protested.

"Yeah, I know, and he'd love to have you here cheering him on every time, but I've just seen what this does to you. Stay home, Lila. Bill won't drop you because you can't handle racing."

"I'll think about it."

"But since you're here today, at least you can participate in the fun part. Let's go congratulate our winner. Can you walk by yourself, do you think? I don't want Bill to think I'm moving in on his territory."

"Yes, I can, and Raphael, you've been terrific. If you can judge a man by his friends, Bill would rank really high."

Raphael smiled. "It works both ways. Bill's the best. I'm glad you two found each other. And don't worry about this racing thing."

Lila knew that she would worry about it. She and Bill had limited time to spend together, and their hobbies didn't seem to match at all. As much as she disliked racing, she couldn't imagine Bill cruising yard sales, either. This was the difficulty, she thought, of bringing two mature people together, people who had already filled their lives and set their patterns, patterns they liked.

As she watched Bill slide into his parking space and climb triumphantly from the car, she sensed how important this racing was to him. She wouldn't spoil it for the world. She hurried forward to give him an enthusiastic victory kiss.

LILA WAS GRATEFUL for the bustle that left no time for talk. People crowded around to inspect the dent made when Bill cut off his opponent. Jack complained halfheartedly about the bodywork that would now be necessary, but Lila could tell he didn't mind a bit, was even proud of Bill for driving so aggressively. Every time she looked at the dent she felt as if someone had put a similar one in her stomach. She'd have to toughen up.

Sweat-soaked and laughing, Bill leaned against the car with one arm around Lila and his free hand holding a cold beer. Lila wanted desperately for it all to be over and for Bill to take her in his arms and love her until the sound of the crash faded from her memory. She wanted to hold him and feel for herself that he was in one piece, undamaged by the wrenching punishment of the race.

The start of the next race thinned out the crowd surrounding the yellow Corvette, and finally Jack suggested they load it onto the trailer. "You gonna stay for anymore races?" Jack asked Bill as the three men secured the car to the flatbed.

"I don't think so," Bill said, and glanced at Lila. "Unless you want to?"

"No, that's okay," she said.

"Because if you're enjoying yourself, we can watch a few more—"

"No, let's go after this race," she said quickly, not wanting to get into any sort of discussion about her questionable enjoyment of the sport.

When the fifth race ended and the track opened for people to leave the pit, Bill and Lila said goodbye to Jack and Raphael, who were staying until the end. Jack said he hoped to see Lila again, but Raphael simply winked and wished her good luck. Lila knew that he didn't think she should return to the track. While she appreciated his understanding attitude, she didn't believe the answer was that simple.

As they walked to the parking lot, Lila thought about Raphael's fine qualities, not to mention his good looks, and she had an inspiration. Raphael was a little young for Penny, but maybe not too young. Besides, the older woman-younger man combination was catching on these days.

"I like your friends," she said to Bill.

"They're nice guys," Bill agreed. "I'd trust them with my life. In point of fact, I do trust them with my life."

"I was thinking about Penny just now," Lila said. "Raphael seems to be a terrific guy, and—"

"And he's married."

"Really?" Lila was disappointed. "But he doesn't wear a ring, and besides, where was his wife?"

"He doesn't wear a ring because he thinks it's dangerous to wear one working as a mechanic. Some guys worry about that. And as for his wife, she hates racing."

"Oh." Lila understood Raphael's words of caution a little better. "What doesn't she like about it?"

"Everything. Some women object to the danger for the drivers, but Raphael doesn't drive—yet. I suppose he will one of these days. But even without the danger to Raphael, Susie doesn't like any of it—the noise, the smell, the heat. They seem to have worked out that problem by her staying home, but I feel a little sorry for Raphael. He can't share his passion for racing and cars with her."

"Oh."

"That's why I loved having you there today. I think I kind of showed off for you."

A chill traveled down her spine. "You mean that last maneuver?"

"Yeah. I wanted to win with you watching. Pretty juvenile, huh?"

She gulped. "Bill—"

"Hey." He squeezed her shoulder. "I don't drive like that very often. I promise."

"That's good," she said, unconvinced. "Well, here's my car."

"Okay. I'm right over there, the black Jag. Just follow me. I'll go slow and make sure you're behind me."

"Fine."

He leaned down to give her a quick kiss. "Thanks for being there today." Then he sprinted for his car before she could respond. She unlocked her car and slid into the warm, dusty interior. He was so hyped up by this racing business, she thought. She couldn't possibly tell him how she really felt, at least not now.

He drove sedately all the way to his house, but she wasn't fooled. She'd just seen him race, and at every stoplight she had to stare at a license plate that spelled out: Gun It! Well, she might have guessed that once she'd moved out of the geek class, as Tracey would describe her former collection of dates, she would end up with someone who scared her to death. Boredom or terror. It didn't seem like much of a choice.

His two-story mission-style house was set against a wooded hill covered with eucalyptus and a few hardwoods. More eucalyptuses, juniper and oleander grew in the neighborhood, making it lush, but cutting off any chance of seeing the horizon. Lila wondered if Bill ever felt closed in. She certainly would if she had to spend more than a weekend here.

There was space for her car in the garage. Apparently he parked the Jag at home and kept the Corvette down where he worked. As she would expect from a mechanic, the garage was immaculate. He could have staged a party there and not worried about someone stepping on any grease. She hoped that her Buick wouldn't leak any oil and embarrass her.

She took her small overnight bag from the seat beside her as he opened her car door. She glanced up at him and smiled.

"Home sweet home," he said, helping her out.

"It's lovely, Bill."

"You're a connoisseur of garages?"

"I meant the house, from the outside, but of course the garage is perfect. I wouldn't expect anything else from a mechanic."

He grimaced. "The house is just as orderly. I have been accused of being an obsessive neatnik."

"Really?" Lila thought of the cabin where they'd first made love, of the clothes strewn over the floor and the dishes from their impromptu supper left carelessly on the dresser, not even put outside the door for the steward to collect.

He took her overnight bag and grabbed her hand. "But the people who accuse me of excessive neatness don't know that under certain circumstances, order is the last thing on my mind," he said, leading her through a door into the kitchen.

"You guessed what I was thinking about."

"I hope you think about it a lot, and the short time we spent together last week, too."

"I do."

He drew her into his arms. "Can I give you the house tour later?"

"You bet, Billy-goat."

He chuckled. "I probably smell like one, too."

"I like the way you smell," she admitted. She didn't mind the scent of car exhaust and oil when they were here, safe in his house, and he was holding her tight.

"Take a shower with me, first," he suggested. "I know you don't need one, but I do."

She kissed him and tasted the salt of his sweat. "You see, you are a neatnik," she teased.

"No, I'm a smart man. I know all the places I want that sweet mouth of yours, and I doubt you'd be as enthusiastic as I want you to be if you're kissing gasoline-scented skin."

"And how do you know that?"

"Before you saw me this morning, I was near the gate, looking for you. I saw this nose—" He paused to kiss her there. "I saw this nose wrinkle, when you didn't know I was watching you, before they opened the gates and you ran across."

"Maybe I had an itch."

"Maybe. But I have one right now, and we might even start scratching it in the shower. Let's go." He swung her up into his arms.

"Goodness, Tarzan," she said, loving every minute of it as he climbed the stairs with her in his arms. "How strong you are."

"Race car drivers have to be athletes, too. It takes muscle to control those cars."

"I'll bet," she said, wishing they'd talk about something else. "You forgot my overnight bag. It's still in the kitchen."

"That's okay. For a few hours, at least, you won't need a thing out of it."

"My, how you talk," she said, nuzzling his neck and settling into the whirling joy of the physical love between them. This was what she'd driven here for, endured the race for—to submerge herself in sensation with Bill.

"I'm only keeping my mouth limber for more important things," he murmured, carrying her through the master suite and into the spacious bathroom. He set her on her feet. "Strip," he said, reaching for the brass-plated faucets in the shower.

"Yes, sir. This is quite a bathroom." She compared it with hers, built before it was popular to have large bathrooms with elaborate fixtures.

"I used to think it was a waste," he said, kicking off his shoes. "But lately I've mellowed. I've even been known to get into the tub and turn on the whirlpool."

"All by yourself?" She pulled her sweater over her head.

"Not always." He gave her a steady look. "Maybe we should deal with this right now. I haven't been a monk since my wife's death, but my reputation stretches far beyond what is actually true about me. And I only have one relationship at a time. You don't have to worry that

I'll spend my weeknights with other women and my weekends with you."

She felt chastened. "I probably didn't have the right to make that remark. I know you're careful about your personal life, and that's really the only—"

"Stop right there." He gripped her arms and brought her close. "Obviously we aren't communicating. I'm serious about what's happening between us. Very serious."

Her pulse hammering, she looked into the hypnotic blue of his eyes. "So am I," she whispered.

"Then raise your expectations."

"I—I don't understand what you mean."

He held her tight and his intense expression underlined every word. "Expect me to honor you by not sleeping with anyone else. Expect me to care for you and cherish what you offer me. Expect me, in short, to love you."

She couldn't speak, couldn't move.

"Does it surprise you that I might?" he asked, his tone gentling.

"I guess...it does," she admitted, struggling to form a thought, much less an answer. "Love wasn't part of the bargain."

A shadow crossed his expression. "I see." He released her and turned away. "Thank God we cleared that up. Sorry if I got maudlin, but I thought—"

"You thought exactly right," she said, touching his arm.

He glanced back at her.

Her smile trembled. "You can expect me, in short, to love you, too."

11

BILL'S ENTHUSIASTIC RESPONSE to Lila's declaration of love made them both forget their plan to shower first. They also dispensed with a bed in favor of the bathroom floor. At the last moment, Bill grabbed a towel to spread under Lila, but she wouldn't have minded the cold press of ceramic tile, so great was her need for him to fill her. Afterward, they lay panting amid the chaos of half-removed clothes and gazed at each other, awed by the force of their passion.

"I do love you," Bill said, still breathing hard.

"And I love you, too."

He glanced around at the mess and grinned. "Apparently." Then he touched her breast. "Some grease from my shirt got on you. That's what I really call love."

"Doesn't matter. I'll wash it off."

"Nice thought. And I'm just the guy to help you do it."

And he accomplished the task quite thoroughly as they stood beneath the warm shower together. He held her steady as his movements with the sudsy washcloth made her pulse with renewed desire. Finally, she wrested the cloth away from him and repaid him in kind, until he had to lean against the shower wall and close his eyes to regain control.

They emerged from the shower clean and aroused, then proceeded to heighten their desire as they slowly rubbed each other dry.

"It's strange," Bill murmured, moving the towel down the inside of her thigh, "but the drier you get here, the damper you get other places."

"I've noticed," she said with a ragged sigh. "And I wonder how you can be so soft and yet so firm." She wrapped her fingers around him. "Right here." She smiled when he sucked in his breath in response. "Nature's mysteries, I guess."

"Let's explore those mysteries on a mattress this time." Bill tossed their towels on the floor and led her into the bedroom.

Emboldened by his words of love, Lila took charge, instructing Bill to lie back and receive what he'd originally asked for when he'd carried her up the stairs—her lips on every inch of him. She skipped nothing and paid special attention where it was due, making him moan with pleasure. Finally, when he warned her he was losing control, she reached for the package on the bedside table.

"I'll—" he said, starting to take the package.

"No, I will," she murmured.

"Be quick," he said, his voice strained.

She wasn't quick, and he groaned and clenched his jaw. Finally, she lowered herself, nearly crying out at the bliss of uniting with the man she loved.

"Lila, you have to believe me," he murmured, gazing up at her. "It's never been like this. Not with anyone."

"I believe you. Because I feel the same way."

"Love me," he urged, grasping her hips.

"Yes." By now she knew the splendor that awaited her, and the knowledge increased her anticipation. She moved with sureness and watched his face until her own response blurred her vision. She felt him quiver and then he called her name as her world erupted in concert with his.

THE ROOM WAS DARK when Lila awoke. Bill slept, no doubt exhausted by his race and their two strenuous lovemaking sessions. Carefully, she slipped from under his encircling arm and eased out of bed. Enough light filtered in from a streetlamp to guide her to a large walk-in closet. With some muted fumbling, she managed to locate one of his bathrobes and put it on. She was hungry and decided to search out something to eat.

She felt her way down the carpeted stairs and didn't turn on a light until she'd reached the first floor. In the living room she tried a wall switch and three lamps came on, two on tables at either end of a leather sofa, and one floor lamp beside a large leather recliner.

She surveyed the decor with a practiced eye. Years of being in real estate had made her a discerning judge of quality and Bill's furniture was definitely that. The gray leather and burgundy accents appealed to her, but he was right about being a neatnik. The room was so uncluttered it was cold. She touched a rubber plant. Fake. The coffee table carried nary an ashtray or magazine.

She wandered through the dining room and into the kitchen, where she could find no fault with the arrangement of appliances or the blue-and-white color scheme. But this room also had the atmosphere of a museum. She sat down at the pine trestle table and finally figured out part of the reason: the place was absolutely still.

There was no ocean to whisper outside, and because Bill lived on a seldom-traveled street, traffic noise was at a minimum. Inside the house, the only living thing to make noise was Bill. With Jason gone, he had no other people to turn on radios and televisions, to whistle, or to bang drawers shut. And he had no pets.

Once she'd noticed the silence, it began to wear on her. She'd go crazy in such quiet if she had to live here. But she didn't have to live here. No one had said anything about that, she reminded herself. In the meantime, she had some control over this oppressive quiet. She located the coffeemaker and coffee, and soon had the gurgle and drip to keep her company. Then, she rummaged through the refrigerator and found some sliced turkey. By the time Bill appeared in the kitchen doorway, she was making sandwiches and humming to herself. She heard his step and glanced up with a welcoming smile.

"Hi," he said, leaning against the doorjamb with one hand behind his back. He'd pulled on tan sweatpants and a sweatshirt.

"Hi, yourself. What are you hiding behind your back?"

"I wondered if you wanted to fiddle around."

"I thought that's what we'd been doing," she said, chuckling.

"Yes, but not like this." From behind his back he brought a violin and bow.

Lila stared, wondering if that was the way he broke the silence of this mausoleum. Never in her wildest dreams would she have guessed that he played a violin.

"Want to hear something?"

She nodded, still wide-eyed.

He began scraping the bow across the strings to create the worst sound she'd heard since Onyx's last fight with a neighbor's cat.

"Stop!" she said, laughing. "Jason won't appreciate your doing that to his violin."

He took the instrument from under his chin. "You're not impressed?" he said with a wounded look. "I was trying to show you that I'm not just another dashing, handsome race car driver."

She shook her head, still laughing. "I love you just the way you are. Now put that down so we can have something to eat."

He positioned the violin under his chin again. "In a minute. Maybe I just need more practice."

"Bill, for heaven's sake. You—" She stopped speaking as a haunting melody came from the carefully stroked strings. Judging from Bill's changed posture and his concentration, this wasn't Jason's instrument. It was Bill's and he certainly knew how to play it. She stood transfixed as he performed a piece she recognized as classical and highly romantic. Never before had a man played for her, *to* her, and she was thoroughly charmed.

He finished and glanced up. "Better?"

"You're an incredible man," she said softly, going to him. "That was beautiful. Does your pit crew know about this?"

He shook his head and laid the violin on the kitchen counter. "I've played ever since I was a kid, but I got teased so much I quit orchestra in high school. I kept my music to myself after that." He laughed. "Some people have skeletons in their closets. I have a violin."

She put her arms around his waist. "Thank you for trusting me with something so private."

"It's nice to feel that I can." He gathered her close. "I know that when we first met the sexual chemistry overwhelmed everything else, but there's more to this attraction than sex. I like you."

She nestled her head in the curve of his shoulder. "I like you, too."

"When I saw you in here making sandwiches, I was impressed by what a nice picture it made. You looked right at home."

She didn't respond. In his arms like this, she felt at home. But in this house, with its fake plants and sterile environment, even with occasional music from his violin, she knew she couldn't feel at home.

"What is it?" He leaned down and brushed his lips against her cheek. "What did I say?" Then he groaned. "I know. You think I'm pleased that you're in the kitchen with the womanly chore of fixing food. Next, you expect me to give you my dirty socks to wash."

She lifted her head and gazed into his eyes. "I hadn't thought of that, to tell the truth. Oh, Bill." She sighed. "We've already become more entangled with each other than we ever intended, and I love the time we spend together, but I think we have to be careful of the assumptions we make. I have my life and you have yours. We said it was important to both of us to keep it that way."

He studied her silently for several seconds. "You're right. Of course you're right." He grinned. "So, as the guest chef in *my* kitchen, what have you made for us?"

"Turkey."

"Don't call me names in my own kitchen."

She laughed, relaxing again.

"That's better," he said, kissing her nose. "Now, my fiercely independent love, let's eat. After that we can fiddle a little more with my bow."

She lifted one eyebrow.

"All double meanings intended," he said, and pinched her bottom.

LILA BEGAN SPENDING most of her weekends at Bill's house. He was willing to come down to see her on those weekends when he didn't race, but she couldn't imagine how they would engineer a carefree romp in bed, one of their favorite activities, with Tracey and little Stevie right down the hall.

Repeated exposure to Bill's racing had calmed Lila's fears to some extent, although she found she had to consciously unclench her jaw each time a race ended. Raphael watched her with an amused expression, but he never told Bill what he knew about her nervousness.

Once in a while, she and Bill met the pit crew and their wives at a restaurant for dinner, and Lila observed the affection between Raphael and his wife. Lila wished for the courage to stay home from the races, as Susie did, but Lila wasn't certain Bill would react with the good humor Raphael showed toward his wife's decision. Besides, Lila reasoned, her time with Bill was limited and giving up the races would mean giving up a big chunk of that time. Unless, of course, she asked him to skip a race now and then, but that, for her, was unacceptable.

She found leaving each Sunday increasingly difficult, knowing that she wouldn't see Bill until the following weekend. She delayed her departure longer each Sunday, often arriving home late in the evening.

As Thanksgiving approached, Bill told her that he would be flying back to Boston to see Jason; they couldn't spend that weekend together unless she wanted to come with him. Lila thought of Tracey and Stevie and knew she couldn't do it. The Sunday before Thanksgiving, Bill coaxed her to stay late on the pretext that they wouldn't be seeing each other for two weeks. Lila's grandfather clock was chiming midnight when she finally put her key in the lock of her front door.

She walked in to find Tracey pacing the floor with Stevie in her arms. "What is it?" Lila asked, crossing quickly to her daughter.

"Do you care?" Tracey asked, continuing to pace.

Lila wanted to spank her. "Of course I care!" she snapped, and turned her attention to Stevie. His eyes were closed, his face flushed. His breathing rasped in the silence. "Sounds like croup. Have you called the doctor?"

"No, because I was waiting for you," Tracey said. "I thought you'd be back any minute, and I didn't want to drive there alone at this time of night, but you didn't come, and didn't come, and—" Tracey began to cry.

"I'll call the doctor. We'll take him to the emergency room," Lila said, hurrying to the telephone. She didn't like the sound of Stevie's breathing and she didn't want to stand around debating her arrival time with Tracey. The girl should have taken matters into her own hands, but she hadn't.

The nearest phone was in the kitchen, and as Lila picked up the receiver she glanced around at the dirty dishes and glasses, the food-encrusted pots and pans. She might attribute the mess to Tracey's distraction since Stevie was sick, except for the fact that Lila had found a similar state of affairs every Sunday when she came home. She'd mentioned it to Tracey, but the situation hadn't improved much. Tonight it was especially bad, and Lila muttered under her breath as she dialed the doctor's emergency number.

Within an hour they'd handled Stevie's problem and he was back in his crib. A humidifier, exhumed from the depths of a closet, poured moisture into the air. The doctor had given Stevie a shot and a bottle of medicine, and at last the infant slept. Tracey and Lila tiptoed quietly out of his room.

"I think I'll go to bed," Tracey said, and started down the hall.

"Wait a minute," Lila said. "Come into the living room for a bit. I have a few things to say." She considered postponing the discussion until morning but was afraid that time would blunt her anger and the impact of her words. She needed the strength anger gave her.

"I'm tired, Mom."

"So am I. This will only take a minute." Lila sat in one of the barrel chairs and waited for Tracey to join her.

Tracey plopped into a chair across from her. "If it's about the crystal paperweight, I'll buy you a new one as soon as I can afford it."

"The paperweight?"

"You know, that little fat bird with the bubbles inside. Stevie got hold of it yesterday and smashed it against the fireplace."

Lila winced. A glance at the coffee table confirmed that the bird, which Penny and her husband had brought back from a trip to Italy long ago, was gone. "Did he cut himself?"

"Miraculously, no. I've moved everything out of reach except the vase of flowers, but that should probably go, too."

Lila had been too intent on the current crisis to notice, but she realized, as she gazed around the room, that she was looking at a lot of bare surfaces. The charm was disappearing from her room. *Her* room, not Tracey's and not Stevie's. She took a deep breath.

"To begin with, Tracey, this isn't about the crystal bird, but we may as well include that. First of all, I have asked you repeatedly to clean the kitchen before I get home on Sunday."

"Stevie was sick." Tracey's eyes narrowed in defense. "I couldn't."

"Stevie wasn't sick last week," Lila reminded her. "It was a mess, then, too. You don't have a job other than watching out for yourself and Stevie. I expect you to clean up after yourself from now on, and to prepare dinner for both of us three nights a week." Lila heard the word "expect" pop out of her mouth and thought of Bill's phrase— *Raise your expectations.* It looked as if she needed to do that with Tracey, too.

Tracey stiffened in her chair. "You're not even here two nights a week," she muttered. "So you only have to fix dinner twice, then."

Lila sighed. She'd had this sort of discussion with her daughters years ago; she'd hoped not to have it again. "Tracey, this is not negotiable. I'm paying for all the dinners and working full time to do so. You're welcome here, but you must do your share."

Tracey stared at her resentfully.

Lila plunged on, now deliberately using the word that she'd been underusing in the past. "And I expect my living room to be returned to its original condition, with all my things in their usual places. You will teach Stevie what he can and cannot touch, and supervise him at all times."

Still Tracey gave her the same hard look.

"You're a grown woman, Tracey. When your child is sick, I expect you to take him to the doctor whether I'm here or not, whether you care to drive this late at night or not."

Tracey's rounded chin jutted forward as bitter words tumbled out of a mouth crinkled up with resentment. "It's easy for you to give orders. You're not stuck at home with a little kid all the time. You see clients, and you have this wonderful guy who takes you places, and treats you nice, and—and—" Tears rolled down Tracey's cheeks and she turned away.

Lila sighed. What she'd once suspected was now obvious. Her daughter was jealous. Her tone softened. "Tracey, when was the last time you heard from Mike?" She realized that she'd lost track of that problem since she'd become involved with Bill.

"Yesterday," Tracey said, sniffing.

"And?"

"He wants me to come home, but Mom, it just won't be the same!" She turned back to Lila, her eyes bright with tears. "I know he doesn't love me as much as he used to, or he wouldn't have been attracted to that other woman. I want a guy who's crazy about me, who sends me flowers, who—"

"Like Bill," Lila said gently, thinking of the roses that had arrived last week. She got up and went over to squeeze herself into the chair with Tracey. Tracey resisted at first, and they barely fit, but finally Tracey gave a watery giggle of surrender and cuddled into Lila's arms the way she used to when she was six.

Lila smoothed her hair and took a steadying breath. "Courtship is fun and exciting, sweetheart, and great for the ego," she murmured, "but it doesn't last forever."

"Don't I know it," Tracey said, snuffling.

"Unfortunately, you're watching me go through that phase with Bill right when you're having troubles with Mike."

"Yeah." Tracey sighed. "Sometimes I wish some cute guy would show up and sweep me off my feet, like Bill did with you."

"Oh, Tracey, no you don't." Lila kissed her daughter's hair. "That would make everything so much more complicated for you. You're married. Decide what you want to do about Mike first. Do you still love him?"

"I wish I didn't."

"But you do." Lila's heart ached with remembered pain. "Do you think he loves you?"

"I don't know."

Lila understood. In Stan's case, however, she'd had far more evidence that he didn't care about her. Lila had no idea what sort of advice to give Tracey. For all Lila knew, Mike was a two-timing jerk who should be kicked out.

"Sarah called today," Tracey mumbled.

"Oh?"

"She wanted to know why she hasn't heard from you recently."

"What did you tell her?" Lila asked, although she could predict the answer.

"I told her you didn't have much time these days, now that you have a boyfriend."

Lila closed her eyes. She could imagine her daughters having a field day with that topic.

"Penny called, too, about nine tonight, to see if you were home yet," Tracey added. "On Saturday, I went yard saling with her because she sounded so lonesome."

Lila swallowed as guilt threaded its way into her thoughts. "I'll call Penny tomorrow," she said. "And Sarah tomorrow night. I'll be home through the Thanksgiving weekend, so we can straighten some of this out, but Tracey, I meant what I said about the kitchen, and meals, and especially Stevie. You've got responsibilities."

Tracey didn't answer, but Lila could almost hear her rebellious thoughts. *So do you*, she wanted to say, and she'd be right. Lila hugged her. "Okay, Trace?"

"Okay," came the grudging response.

"Now let's both of us get some sleep."

They hugged again and Tracey went down the hall to bed. Lila locked up the house before heading for her own room. Despite her exhaustion, she lay awake and listened to the clock chime one and then two o'clock.

This moment had been coming for weeks, but she hadn't wanted to believe it. Tracey, Sarah and Penny were only part of what she'd been neglecting recently. By being gone every weekend, she was unavailable to her sales staff, and inevitably the screwups were happening. Real estate was often a weekend business, and sales people who wanted to consult with her about pending deals hadn't been able to do so until Monday. By then, it was often too late to easily correct a fouled-up situation.

In addition, Lila found less and less energy to deal with the mounting problems. Much as she loved spending time with Bill, the drive back and forth took its toll, and the racing frazzled her nerves. Bill's house didn't relax her, and she wasn't spending enough time in her own to relax. Chores that she had been used to handling on the weekends were now crammed into lunch hours or after work, and there was never enough time for anything, even to call Sarah or her best friend.

Lila realized with a pang that she missed the lazy afternoons of yard saling with Penny. She missed walks along the sea cliffs alone, and quiet evenings reading a book with one of the cats in her lap. Onyx and Pearl had become strangers—they seemed to hang around Tracey more than her now.

But Lila had no solution. Being with Bill, making love with him, talking, laughing, had become as necessary to her as breathing. How could she cut back on their already limited time together? She didn't know. Finally, she fell into a restless sleep and awoke a few hours later to the buzz of the alarm and a pounding headache.

By the time Bill called that night, she'd mended a few fences at work and talked with both Sarah at Bryn Mawr and Penny, who was leaving on another trip right after Thanksgiving. Her headache, however, had never entirely disappeared.

"You sound tired," Bill said.

"I am." Lila massaged her temples. "I think I'm too old for this wild life we've been leading."

Bill laughed. "Is that my sex kitten talking?"

"Nope. She's buried under a mound of cat litter."

"Tell me about it."

Lila started to tell him about Tracey's latest bout of jealousy but thought better of it. Ever since the cruise, when he'd been all too ready to advise her about her daughters, Lila had been leery of discussing family problems with him. Instead, she focused on her troubles with the agency. "Work is kind of a hassle these days," she said. "I can't seem to get caught up."

"Will staying home over Thanksgiving help any?"

"Some. But I guess being gone every weekend takes its toll, much as I hate to admit that."

He greeted her statement with silence. At last he spoke. "What do you want to do?"

"I don't know, Bill. I love driving up to see you, but then I turn myself inside out all week trying to juggle my commitments."

"I've worried about that, too, but you always said everything was under control."

"I know. There's a chance I may have been kidding myself." Lila sighed and leaned back in her desk chair. Tears of frustration welled in her eyes.

"Look, do what you can this weekend, and instead of coming up here next weekend, I'll drive down. There's no race, and you can stay home and relax while I make the commute."

"Bill, that's no good. Tracey and Stevie—"

"Don't worry about Tracey and Stevie. I won't stay at your house. But I will take you out to dinner, and afterward we can go to my hotel for a couple of hours. How does that sound?"

"Silly. If I drove up there, we could have the whole weekend."

"And you'd be back to your exhausting schedule. No, let's try this, Lila. And in the meantime, while I'm in Boston, I'll brainstorm other solutions. We can't have you running yourself ragged."

"Oh, it's not really that bad. I just—"

"Hush, now. Don't argue. We'll work on this. And I love you."

"I love you, too."

After she hung up the phone, Lila turned off the lights in her study and opened the shutters to look out at the ocean. Even in November the scuba divers with their green lights bobbed around in the cove. She watched the lights flicker until her body relaxed, as it always did when she took the time to take in her tranquil environment.

She'd protested Bill's plan of driving down and staying in a hotel, but the thought of not having to make the trip herself brought her a calming sense of relief. They wouldn't have the same measure of privacy if he came to La Jolla, but at least she wouldn't have to trade her beloved coastline for the confining trees of Bill's neighborhood. Perhaps he'd hit upon a reasonable compromise, after all.

The thought crossed her mind that if Tracey and Stevie weren't living with her, the whole scenario with Bill would be easier, but they were living with her and she wasn't about to kick them out. A vague uneasiness assailed her as she wondered what "solutions" Bill might suggest. He'd given his opinion about Tracey's presence before and they'd nearly fought about it. Lila hoped he wouldn't put pressure on that sore subject again. If he did, she was afraid he would be risking all that they'd created for themselves.

12

BILL HAD THE SOLUTION to Lila's problem in his pocket, but it made him more nervous than if he'd suddenly been given the chance to drive the Indy 500. He'd treated her to dinner at the Marine Room in La Jolla, figuring she'd enjoy the view of the surf only a few feet from the large restaurant windows. He'd made his room reservation at the adjoining La Jolla Beach and Tennis Club for the same reason. He thought the proximity of the ocean might remind Lila of the cruise, and he needed all the atmosphere he could get.

He'd never seen her look more radiant as she turned to him in the privacy of his hotel room and began to unbutton the blue jersey dress she'd worn to dinner.

"I have a gift for you," she said. "Maybe it will make up for your having to drive down here and stay in a hotel."

"You're gift enough," he said, responding quickly, as he always did, to the creamy seduction of her body.

She allowed the dress to slither to the floor with a delicious whisper, leaving her clad in a pale blue camisole and slip. "About that gift I have for you. I'm taking birth control pills now," she said. "You won't have to use anything."

His heartbeat quickened at the thought of sliding into her unhindered, of experiencing her completely at last. "That's very nice," he said, his voice husky. He fumbled through the removal of his own clothes while he watched her whisk the camisole over her head. Her breasts lifted with the motion and her nipples tipped upward irresistibly. As he hurried through the rest of his task, his mouth moistened with the remembered taste of her.

Lila shimmied out of her slip and panties and stretched out on the bed. Seconds later he joined her and covered her rose-scented, petal-soft skin with kisses. Anticipation made his blood pound through his veins. He wanted to drown in her, and her "gift" would now make it possible. Unable to hold back, he moved between her thighs. "It's been two weeks, and I should take more time with you," he murmured, apologetic but needy.

Her dark eyes were warm, her lips smiling. "Go for it," she whispered.

He didn't need a second invitation. The groan of satisfaction as he buried himself within her came from deep in his soul. He'd kidded himself that the other way of protection was perfectly okay, but nothing, absolutely nothing, felt like this. He luxuriated in the freedom. "Thank you," he murmured, his lips close to her ear.

In answer, she pressed upward, locking them more securely together. In that moment, he was no longer afraid of what the evening would bring. They belonged with each other. They always would. Nothing was more certain to him than that.

As he moved within her, the sweet friction made his response nearly uncontrollable. "I'll have to get used to this," he said, breathing heavily.

"We'll have fun while you do." She pulled his head down for a prolonged kiss.

He managed to hang on to his control, somehow, until he knew she was ready to ride the heights of ecstasy with him. Then he let go, pouring his love into her, absorbing her convulsions as she took what he offered.

"I love your gift," he murmured against her throat when he could talk again. "I love you, come to think of it."

"Good." She hugged him tight. "Because I love you, too."

He lay quietly, savoring the pleasure. At last he remembered, foggily, that he had some things to say to her. Now might be the time. Reluctantly, he left the warmth of her body.

"Where are you going?" she asked. "I thought you'd also like the benefit of not having to get out of bed right away."

"I do. I will." He walked over to his crumpled clothes. "But I have a gift for you, too."

She propped herself up on one elbow as he returned to the bed. He loved looking at her when she was like this, all tousled and rosy from their shared passion.

"I told you I'd think of possible solutions for taking the hassle out of your life. Here's my best shot." He held out a velvet box.

Her eyes widened and she scrambled to a sitting position. She took the box, opened it and found herself staring at a diamond solitaire. Then she glanced up, a million questions in her eyes.

"I know what we said on the cruise, but Lila, this is the only thing that makes sense. We love each other and want to be together. This isn't about my wanting unpaid household help, or you wanting a resident mechanic. We'd be marrying for the right reasons this time around."

"But—but I don't see how this solves anything," she stammered.

He sat on the bed. "I've thought it all out. You can sell your agency in La Jolla and go to work for somebody in Mission Viejo. It would be a lot less responsibility for you. We'll live in my house, and if you're not ready to sell yours because of Tracey, you could let her live in it a while longer. We wouldn't need the money at this point, and the place will continue to go up in value. After Tracey moves out, you can sell or rent, whichever seems most logical at the time." He sat back and waited for her response, which he was sure would be a positive one.

"My God, you're serious."

"You bet I'm serious." He didn't hear wholehearted approval in her answer, but he barreled on. "I hate the strain you've been under recently. I never thought I'd marry again, but now that the idea has occurred to me, I'm nuts about it. So, what do you say? I can see this comes as a shock, but give yourself a chance to get used to it, and you'll love the idea, too. We can even write into the marriage vows that I'll do all my own laundry, if that helps."

She looked as if he'd hit her over the head with the nearest chair. "Laundry is the least of my concerns. Bill, do you realize what you're proposing?"

"I think I'm proposing marriage."

"Not just marriage. You're suggesting I dump the agency I've spent five years rebuilding after Stan almost ruined it. You're asking me to leave a house I love and expecting me to move into one that I..." She broke eye contact with him. "Let's say I don't feel as comfortable in your house as in mine."

He didn't like the way this discussion was going. "What don't you like about my house? We'll change it, redecorate. I could care less about that."

She glanced back at him and her voice was soft. "Would you move your house to a cliff overlooking the ocean?"

"Mission Viejo doesn't have any locations like that. It's too far inland."

"I know. That's a disadvantage for me."

"I never realized you put such a premium on being near the water."

She stared at the ring inside the velvet box before looking up at him. "There are lots of things we haven't talked about, things that didn't seem important as long as we left our situation as it was."

A hard knot formed in his gut. "Are you saying that living by the ocean means more to you than I do?"

"Of course not! How dare you reduce it to those terms?"

"What else am I supposed to think?"

"Maybe nothing, considering your gender." Her eyes filled with the light of battle he remembered from that first night on the cruise. "It seems that when the subject of marriage comes up, the woman is expected to make all the changes. Did you even consider selling *your* business and moving in with me?"

"No."

"Why not?"

He hesitated. There were so many reasons. He'd start with the least volatile. "For one thing, my business depends on repeat customers more than yours. I imagine it would take me much longer to build up my clientele in a new town than it would take you to do the same."

"Possibly, but if you also sold your house, you could ride out the adjustment period, especially with my income to buffer us economically. Or do you have some macho hang-up about being supported by a woman?"

"I don't know. I've never had to find out." He fought against anger. He didn't want this to end in an argument, but it sure had all the signs of going that way. "There are other reasons why I wouldn't want to move down here," he ventured. "I . . . I'm not crazy about living right next to the ocean. It's foggy. It's—it's damp."

Her response sounded lonely and sad. "I'm not crazy about living in the middle of all those trees, either."

He gazed at her. "Seems we haven't been very honest with each other about our preferences, have we?"

"Our preferences weren't an issue before."

"Maybe they don't have to be now," he said gently, taking her hand. "Maybe we could find a compromise house, one without so many trees, and spend lots of vacation time on the ocean."

"Oh, Bill." Her forehead creased. "At the risk of sounding stubborn—I can't give up my house. I dreamed of having one like it all my life. The ocean affords me such serenity, and the occasional vacation just wouldn't do it. Couldn't you reconsider living there?"

"I don't know." Here came the touchy part. "Maybe I could, if . . ." How he hated bringing this one up. "Lila, your house is already kind of . . . crowded."

She grew very still. "You mean because of Tracey and the baby."

"I'm not ready to take that on, Lila."

"I see." Her expression hardened. "You never have approved of that arrangement. How convenient if you simply maneuvered me out of the house."

"Be realistic. Can you really imagine me moving in with you and still having the kind of relationship we enjoy? Not to mention the resentment I'd feel because I don't think Tracey has any business just living off you, and—"

"That's enough." Lila put the ring box on the sheets between them and got out of bed. "Maybe I'd better go home before we both say things we regret."

"Lila, wait." He caught her arm. "Look, I haven't even asked if there's a chance your daughter is planning to reconcile with her husband. I should have asked that first. This argument could be for nothing, for all I know."

"I've heard nothing about reconciliation. I'm unsure about Tracey's plans. And Sarah's, for that matter. She's not doing well at school this semester and she's even talked about coming back home. So you see, Bill, my house will continue to be crowded for some time to come. And I have no intention of moving into yours to ease conditions." She withdrew her arm from his grasp.

Frustration drove him to say the one thing he'd vowed not to say. "Lila, I think those girls are running your life." He saw her recoil, but he'd opened up the subject and he might as well say it all. "You're sacrificing your own well-being for theirs. Don't you and I deserve happiness as much as your daughters?"

She began jerking on her clothes. "Before I met you I had happiness, happiness I had created for myself, without depending on a man to provide it. I vowed never again to think that in order to be happy I would need a man." She buttoned her dress and reached for her shoes. "You see, Bill, the very thing I feared has happened. We became involved, and now things are getting sticky. Neither of us wants to alter our lives to suit the other. We've become two independent, separate people."

"Who happen to love each other!"

She picked up her coat and purse. "Does that mean we have to give away chunks of ourselves in the name of that love?"

"Lila—"

"I'm sorry, Bill." Tears made damp paths down her cheeks. "We've had some great times together."

Fear chilled him. "Don't talk like that. Tomorrow we'll have breakfast. I have the room until eleven. We can—"

She shook her head. "The more you talk the more I understand what has to be done. If we go on, we'll only hurt each other...even more." A sob escaped from her and she hurried for the door. "Goodbye, Bill."

He sat on the bed, stunned into immobility. He couldn't believe that she'd end it like this. Not after the way she'd made love to him moments ago. She loved him, for God's sake! And he loved her, more than he'd admitted even to himself. The anesthetizing effect of his initial shock was wearing off, and in its place throbbed a pain so intense it scared him. What had he done to her? What had he done to himself?

ALL THROUGH THE month of December Lila felt like the glass ornaments hanging from the Christmas tree. She sparkled on the outside, but inside she was hollow, the slightest blow threatening to crush her into a million sharp fragments. Bill called often at first, but as she continued to insist they should end their affair, he gradually stopped calling.

Sarah arrived home from college full of complaints about her professors. She played with Stevie, went shopping with Tracey and went to movies with her old high school friends who were also home for the holidays. She did not, Lila noticed, keep her room clean or offer to help with housework.

Lila threw herself into the usual frenzy of buying gifts and attending parties. Word had circulated that she wasn't seeing "the man from Mission Viejo" any longer, and one of her former dates invited her out. She went, had a miserable time, and came home early.

On Christmas morning, she and the girls sat in the living room in their bathrobes amidst a blizzard of torn wrapping paper and ribbons. It had been an elaborate Christmas, Lila mused, largely subsidized by her paycheck. Stan had sent a few trinkets for the girls and the baby, but most of the clothes, electronic gadgets and toys spilling from boxes scattered around the tree were products of Lila's shopping trips.

Tracey and Sarah sprawled on the floor and discussed what they should do on New Year's Eve, while Stevie sat in the middle of the mess alternately shredding paper and stuffing it into his mouth.

Lila watched him for a short while and finally reached out to take away the piece of red foil he was about to eat. He whimpered and reached for the paper.

"No, Stevie. No good," she said, and handed him the Raggedy Andy doll she'd bought him. "Tracey, I don't think he should chew on the paper. Let's clean it up."

"Okay." Tracey agreed, but immediately returned to her conversation with Sarah.

Lila started gathering paper into an empty box, but she paused when she realized neither of her daughters had moved a muscle to help. "Tracey, Sarah, would you please work on this mess?"

Sarah glanced up. "Sure, Mom." She scooped up whatever was nearest to her and handed it to Lila. "Here you go."

Lila's control snapped. "On your feet, both of you, and police this area! I'm going to get dressed, and when I return, I want every scrap of paper in the garbage."

"Gee, Mom, don't get paranoid," Sarah said, giving Tracey a questioning look. Tracey shrugged.

"I'm not paranoid. I'm tired," Lila said, and walked away. When she reached the hall, she heard them begin talking in low tones. Their words were obscured by the crackle of paper, but Lila knew they were talking about her. Maybe it was about time.

She stood in the shower and thought about the years since the divorce. In those years she'd focused on two things—the happiness of her children and the integrity of her business. She was proud of what she'd accomplished: the girls didn't seem blighted by the divorce and the agency had an excellent reputation for fairness with clients and employees alike.

But Lila had spoken the truth a moment ago. She was tired. She supervised the agents in her office closely, afraid that if she didn't, something might go awry. Perhaps, just perhaps, she needed to delegate some of that responsibility to others. She had good people who could be trusted with more independence. The thought of loosening the reins scared the devil out of her, but she felt liberated, too. The new year would begin soon. It was a good time for a policy change.

And there was the matter of her daughters. Bill's words had been haunting her for days as she watched the self-absorbed behavior of those two girls. They seemed to think that Lila's sole function was to be the cushion that would keep them from landing with too much impact on the hard surface of life. And why not, she thought. She'd seen herself that way until lately, when her job as cushion began squashing her flat. She'd been so on guard against male domination that she hadn't noticed how her own offspring had her jumping through hoops.

Her one attempt to reverse the trend, her one display of backbone, hadn't been a terrific success. After the night Stevie had suffered that attack of croup, Tracey had returned the original decor to the living room, but she hadn't watched Stevie carefully enough and he'd uprooted and torn apart one of Lila's cherished ivy plants. Tracey did cook dinner three times a week as agreed, although Lila often gave in and helped; furthermore, because Lila was home on weekends now, Tracey never was alone long enough to create a mound of dirty dishes in the kitchen.

Lila dried off from the shower and dressed in a purple jumpsuit. It was a strong color and she needed strength today.

By the time she returned to the living room, it had been tidied up and both girls were in the kitchen. Lila joined them. "Looks as though breakfast is in progress," she said with a smile.

"That's right." Tracey blew on a small piece of toast and handed it to Stevie, who was banging on his high chair with a spoon. "You just relax, Mom. Sarah and I will serve you this morning."

"How nice." Lila sat at the kitchen table next to Stevie's high chair and used his bib to wipe some drool from his chin. She watched Sarah scrambling eggs and saw herself at that age. Sarah had inherited Lila's brunette coloring, while Tracey looked more like Stan.

"Here's some juice," Tracey said, placing a glass in front of Lila.

"Thank you, Tracey." Lila's eyes misted as she studied her daughters. Perhaps she'd been too harsh in her judgment. They were sweet girls at heart, and they were, after all, still young.

They presented breakfast with a flourish and Lila praised the effort.

"It's the least we could do," Sarah said. "More coffee?"

"Please." Lila congratulated herself. Apparently one well-timed declaration had done the job. "When's Mike coming by, Tracey?"

Tracey grimaced. "Do we have to talk about him?"

"Well, he is Stevie's father, and it is Christmas. I'm sure Mike wants to bring him something. Perhaps he even has a gift for you, Trace."

"Stevie might not even recognize him, you know," Tracey observed. "Besides, Sarah and I have it all worked out. After Mike's been here an hour, we'll announce that we have to go to Penny's, and that Stevie's coming with us. That'll break things up nicely."

Lila frowned. "That seems pretty cruel to Mike, Tracey. I thought you still had some feeling for him."

Tracey handed Stevie another piece of toast. "I've been thinking about that. You know, trying to figure out the difference between love and infatuation. Now I wonder how much I cared about him in the first place. It seemed like a neat idea, to get married, have my own house, my own baby. But it wasn't as fun as I thought it would be."

Sarah nodded. "I told you marriage would confine you, Trace. But you wouldn't listen."

Lila put down her fork and leaned toward Tracey. "Tracey, this isn't like the car you bought. You can't just decide it's not a great idea and trade it in. You have a child. Mike is his father. You're messing around with this little person's life."

Stevie crowed and crammed another section of toast into his mouth.

"Lots of kids grow up without both parents," Tracey said. "Besides, you're a wonderful grandmother. Maybe Stevie's better off being raised by women. Maybe he'll pick up more of the feminist—"

"Tracey, you sound as if you mean to live here forever!" Lila said, aghast.

Tracey stared at her. "Well, of course not *forever*, but Mom, you have plenty of room, so what's the big deal?"

Lila started to shake. So she'd thought that these girls had understood her, had she? Apparently much more needed to be said. She braced both hands on the table and prepared to say it. "Look, both of you." She gazed into Tracey's blue eyes and Sarah's brown ones. "This may come as a shock, but I have a life, too. When you were babies, it was necessary for me to subjugate my needs to yours, but you're not babies any longer."

"We know that," Sarah said impatiently. "But sometimes you treat us that way, like telling us to pick up the papers this morning."

"You're right," Lila agreed. "I shouldn't be speaking to you that way. I shouldn't have to, not at your age. Here's the way I should speak to you. Sarah, you've been hinting that you might drop out of college. That's entirely up to you, but if you chose to do that, you will find yourself a job and an apartment. You will not come home to live here, off the fat of the land."

Sarah's dark eyes flashed. "But Tracey—" she began.

"That's the other part," Lila said, turning to her eldest daughter. "Tracey, I gave you a place to stay because I assumed you needed a temporary haven where you could lick your wounds. I never expected this to be a permanent, or even semipermanent arrangement. Whether you go back to Mike is your decision, as is Sarah's to stay in college. You have two weeks from today to make that decision. If you choose not to return to your marriage, you must find a job and an apartment. I need my privacy back." Lila waited, her heart pounding. Both girls looked stricken, and a part of her wanted to recant every word. She subdued that part.

"Well, some Christmas this is!" Tracey said, leaving the table and unsnapping the tray from Stevie's high chair. "I never expected such treatment from my own mother."

Apologies rose to Lila's lips, but she swallowed them.

"Privacy for what?" Sarah asked, her chin stuck out in defiance. "Some guy?"

"No," Lila said. "For myself."

"Ha," Tracey said, juggling Stevie on one hip. "I'll bet she wants to move that race car driver in here, Sarah. I never did believe he was gone for good."

"It's not because of Bill," Lila said, and knew the moment she said it that it was true. Somewhere in all of this she'd lost her beloved, replenishing solitude. She didn't want Bill here full time any more than she wanted Tracey or Sarah around on a constant basis. "And both of you are welcome for short visits, but it's time for you to be on your own, both of you. My mothering days are over."

Sarah rose from her chair. "Well, Trace, she's flipped. That's all there is to it. Maybe it's a phase."

"Don't count on it," Lila said, as the two girls stomped away to hash over the new state of affairs.

Lila sat at the table sipping her coffee. Guilt threatened to overwhelm her, but she fought it with all the willpower she possessed. She reminded herself of Tracey's nonchalant statement about Stevie being raised among women, specifically a "loving grandmother." She reminded herself of Sarah's intelligence, brainpower she was squandering because she was too lazy to buckle down and study. Lila reminded herself that both girls always seemed to take the easy way out, if Lila allowed them to. In their interests, as well as hers, she could no longer allow it.

The doorbell rang. She didn't think Mike was due this soon. She was sure something had been said about his arriving in the afternoon. She went to the door and discovered a radiant Penny on the other side, holding out her left hand.

"Penny, my Lord, it's a ring!" Lila ushered her friend inside while still holding her hand and gazing at the large diamond on her fourth finger. "But who?"

"Fred, my travel agent." Penny's whole body was smiling. "He proposed last night. I know the girls are coming over later, but I couldn't wait. I had to drive over and show you."

Lila laughed and hugged her. "Your travel agent. What a riot. I didn't even know he was single."

"Neither did I." Penny sat in a chair and held her hand out; the diamond flashed in the light. "Seems all this time he was sending me on husband-hunting trips, he was working up his courage to ask me out."

"But how many dates have you had? I didn't even realize that—"

"Just two," Penny admitted. "That's all it took. I would have told you about the dates, but everything's been so hectic, with the kids home, and Christmas, that I decided to wait and have a long gab session with you after the holidays. But then things started moving so fast, and . . ." She grinned. "Here I am, engaged."

"To your travel agent," Lila said, still marveling. "But Penny, I don't remember that Fred's physique is all that wonderful."

"I, um, discovered something," Penny admitted with a gleam in her eye. "Sometimes a guy who isn't built like Adonis tries a little harder to please."

"I love it," Lila said, laughing. "Oh, Penny, only you would end up with a marvelous story like this."

Penny's smile faded. "You could, too, Lila. I know you don't want to talk about it, but I'm so happy, that I can't help thinking about—"

"Never mind. That's over."

"Look, some day Tracey and Sarah will be out of the picture. Then you'll look around and find you're alone."

Lila lowered her voice. "That will happen sooner than you think, Penny. I sounded off to both girls this morning. I've told Sarah that she can stay in college or leave, but if she leaves she's on her own."

"No kidding?" Penny gazed at Lila with new respect. "I'm impressed. What about Tracey?"

"She's got two weeks notice. She can patch things up with Mike or find a job and an apartment."

"Sakes alive, honey, you've done it. Good for you."

"What I haven't told them is that once they've begun the struggle to be self-sufficient, I'll still help them financially if they're desperate."

"Make it a loan," Penny advised. "I think you've had an open hand long enough."

"You're right. Maybe now my help should be in the form of loans."

"So, Lila, doesn't this clear the way?" Penny moved forward in her chair. "Couldn't you and Bill . . . you know, work something out?"

Lila gazed at her friend. "I don't think so. We can't go back to what we had, now that he's brought marriage into the picture."

"Then marry him, you silly woman! I'll bet you could talk him into moving into this house with you and opening a new garage in La Jolla. Shoot, we could all work hard to bring him business. Think what fun we could have, with you and Bill, me and Fred—"

"Penny, I don't want him moved into this house. He wouldn't like it, for one thing. He's not crazy about the ocean, and it seems a waste for someone who doesn't appreciate the location to live full time in this house."

"Can you possibly live in Mission Viejo, then? I'd hate to lose you, but it's only an hour and a half drive. We'd still see lots of each other, and I'm sure you could sell real estate up there."

Lila shook her head. "That's no good, either. I'd resent giving up my ocean views, and besides, I don't want to leave the agency. Especially not now, when I have some new ideas about how to run it."

Penny's shoulders slumped. "This is dumb. You two would be so happy together. I can't—" She stopped and snapped her fingers. "Wait a minute! This is the modern age. Why do either of you have to choose? Why can't you trade off weekends in each place, and spend the weeks in your own homes?"

"And be married?"

"Why not?"

"Because in marriage, you live together, that's why not. You and Fred will live together, right?"

"Yes, but we don't have your problem. We both like my place."

"Penny, this is one of the craziest ideas you've ever come up with, and that's saying something."

"Try it on Bill. See how crazy it is."

Lila's pulse accelerated. "Oh, Penny, I don't know. I haven't heard from him in two weeks. He might not want to talk with me at all."

"Guess again. He called me yesterday to see how you were."

"He did?"

"Lila, he's nuts about you. Call him today. Make his Christmas complete."

"I couldn't suggest this plan over the phone."

"Then don't. Arrange to meet him somewhere. Somewhere private."

Lila trembled at the thought of talking to Bill. She'd thrown his marriage proposal back in his face. She had no idea how he'd react to this new idea. It sounded ridiculous, even to her. "Okay, I'll think about it," she said.

13

LILA KEPT THE THOUGHT of calling Bill to herself, as if it were a treasure map in a secret drawer. At quiet moments throughout the remainder of Christmas day, she'd contemplate making the call and feel both shivery and warm. She'd decided to call him after nine o'clock, when Stevie was in bed, and the house had quieted down. He might not be home, of course. He even might be out with a woman. Lila refused to think much about that.

Mike arrived to see Stevie, and he brought presents for everyone, including a diamond pendant for Tracey. Tracey's attitude toward her husband seemed improved, so much so that she invited him to stay for Christmas dinner. Lila wondered if her ultimatums over the breakfast table had anything to do with Tracey's changed approach.

Mike left soon after dinner, but Lila glimpsed a quick embrace on the front porch before he drove away. She smiled to herself. She didn't know if Tracey and Mike would make a go of their marriage, but at least now that she'd withdrawn her support, they'd be forced to try. Funny how the decision to help herself also seemed to have helped them. At least now they'd move off dead center and take action, one way or the other.

After Mike left, Tracey and Sarah joined Lila in clearing the table and loading the dishwasher. Lila was congratulating herself once again on having made progress, as the three women worked congenially through the dirty dishes and leftover food.

"Mike asked me out for New Year's Eve," Tracey said, glancing at Lila for a reaction.

"Wonderful," Lila said.

"I figured you'd like that," Tracey said.

"What did you say?" Sarah asked.

"That I'd think about it."

"What about that party we were invited to?" Sarah continued. "Of course, I suppose you could bring Mike. There won't be many married people there, but I guess that doesn't matter."

As Lila listened to the discussion, a warning flashed in her mind. "You two already have plans for New Year's Eve?" she asked casually.

"Sure," Sarah replied. "You know, the same old gang usually gets together, kids from school, some of our old friends from the neighborhood. John's having it this year because his folks are in the Bahamas." She glanced at Lila. "You're not going to gripe about chaperons, are you?"

"No. I gave that up after you graduated from high school. What I'm concerned about is a babysitter for Stevie."

Both girls looked at her with their mouths open, confirming what she'd suspected. They had assumed she would take care of Stevie while they partied all night. Apparently, years of indoctrination wouldn't be erased by one firmly stated speech at breakfast.

Tracey recovered first. "I'd think you'd be glad to sit for him, Mom. I'll be out with Mike, after all."

"But Mike wasn't part of the original plan," Lila reminded her. "You two just assumed I'd be home to take care of Stevie, didn't you?"

"But Mom," Sarah protested, "it's not like you're involved with anyone now that the race car driver is history. You said yourself that the guys you've dated are nerds, so where would you want to go on New Year's Eve?"

Lila thought about Bill, about bringing in the New Year together in each other's arms. Where would she want to go, indeed. These two hadn't the foggiest notion of her fantasies.

"Hey, Mom, you have a weird look on your face," Sarah commented. "What's going on?"

"I don't know yet," Lila said, drying her hands on a dish towel and hanging it on the rack by the stove. "But I would advise you, Tracey, to hunt up a sitter for Stevie on New Year's Eve. In fact, don't count on me for babysitting anymore without asking first. I might have plans."

"Plans?" Tracey repeated, looking mystified.

"I can tell this concept bears repeating," Lila said without rancor. Now that her way was clear, she no longer needed anger to underscore her point. "I am a person with a life of my own. I'd like both of you to respect that and not make assumptions about what I'm willing to do for you. Now if you'll excuse me, I have a phone call to make."

She smiled as she went down the hall to her study. They were floored by her new behavior, but they'd adapt soon enough; they were intelligent girls capable of consideration for her once she'd shown them what that meant.

Lila closed the door to her study and turned out the light. Walking deliberately past the Garfield phone to the window, she opened the shutters and gazed out at the whispering sea. No phosphorescent lights tonight. Perhaps the divers had made a concession to Christmas, she thought, leaning her forehead against the cool glass. She wondered what Bill was doing right now. Jason might be there. Perhaps others were, too, maybe even Raphael and Jack and their wives and children.

Lila thought of Penny's audacious suggestion that she and Bill marry and maintain two households. If they ever managed such a feat, she wondered how they'd handle holidays. Her daughters had never celebrated anywhere but here. She had no idea what traditions Bill had cultivated over the years. Lila sighed. None of this was going to be simple, assuming it even had a chance of success.

Yet Bill had called Penny only yesterday and asked about Lila. He still cared. Lila couldn't turn her back on that. She'd declared to her daughters that she had a life of her own, and now the burden of proof was on her. She wanted Bill to be part of that life, somehow. Leaving the window, she walked back to her desk and picked up the telephone receiver. Garfield's eyes opened.

Jason answered on the third ring, and Lila could hear laughter and the clink of dishes in the background. She identified herself and was gratified at Jason's enthusiastic response before he put down the phone to go find his father. A door closed, blocking out the noise, and rapid footsteps approached the phone.

"Lila?" Bill sounded boyishly eager.

"Merry Christmas, Bill," Lila said, almost unable to speak as emotion crowded her throat.

"Merry Christmas to you." His voice was low, gentle. "I've thought about you all day."

"I've thought about you, too. Penny told me you called yesterday."

"I told her not to tell you, unless—"

"Bill, I do want to see you again." She heard his deep sigh and longed to hold him and soothe away all the hurt they'd caused each other. "I want to try and work something out."

"You don't know how I've longed to hear that."

"Maybe I do. Listen, the most important thing you should know is that you were right about Tracey. Sarah fell into the same category, for that matter. I'm in the process of cutting the apron strings, Bill. It took me a while to face the truth of what you'd said, and I—I guess I was pretty angry with you for saying what I didn't want to hear. I'm sorry."

"As you recall, I tried about twenty times to take back what I'd said."

"You can't take back something like that. Especially when it hits so close to home. Maybe if you hadn't said it, I wouldn't have realized what I've been doing to those girls. I've been robbing them of the chance to grow up, Bill."

"Hey, don't be so hard on yourself. You've also given them tons of love. You've done what you thought best. Nobody can ask for more than that."

Lila basked in the sound of his voice. "I've missed you so much."

"Likewise. When do we get to end this torture? Just say the word and I'll be in my car."

She laughed, feeling giddy. "Tomorrow's a workday for me, and I'll bet for you, too."

"I can cancel."

"I can't. Let's not get crazy, here. But what are you doing New Year's Eve, as the song goes?"

"Whatever I was doing, it's all canceled as of this minute."

"You had a date," she said, her stomach twisting.

"Raphael and Jack found me someone. I told them I didn't want to, but they refused to tune the 'Vette if I said no."

"I don't want to mess up people's plans," Lila said, feeling miserable.

"Now wait a minute. I don't know this lady, and I'm in love with you. I'll find her another date myself, if necessary, okay?"

"Okay." Lila's joy returned.

"Your place or mine? No, I take that back. We'd better make it mine. There's a race New Year's Eve day. You can come up for that, and then we'll have the whole evening to ourselves. If you want my vote, we won't go out at all."

Lila took a deep breath. She'd found the strength to be straight with the girls. Now it was time to be straight with the man she loved. "I think I'll come up after the race," she said.

"After? Why, do you have something else to do?"

"No. But you see...the races aren't...they aren't my thing. I'm petrified that you'll be in a crash, and although you could still be in one whether I'm there or not, I can block out the possibility more without the screech of tires to remind me." She waited through several seconds of agonizing silence. "I should have told you before," she added, nervously twisting the telephone cord.

"How about if I don't race that day?" he said at last. "We'll have more time together then."

"No, please don't do that. I want you to race. At least, the mature part of me wants you to. Don't you see? We have to build a relationship that doesn't include sacrificing what we enjoy. So, you should have the freedom to race cars and I should have the freedom not to watch."

"Why didn't you tell me before?"

"For the same reason I didn't stand up for myself with my daughters. I wanted to make you happy."

"Oh, lady, you can do that in better ways than watching me race. If you were here right now I'd demonstrate."

Lila felt warm all over. "But you talked about Raphael's wife as if you thought she was terrible for staying away."

He hesitated. "I guess I'm guilty. Okay, sure, I'd love to have you enjoy racing the way I do. But after this bout of being away from you, I've gained some perspective, too."

"That's good," Lila said, knowing he'd need an open mind for what she would propose. "Because we have lots to discuss and decide."

"As long as we start from the idea of being together, I can handle anything."

Lila hoped so. "Then I'll see you New Year's Eve afternoon," she said.

"Wait. I've just had a brainstorm. Can you get away earlier, maybe the night before?"

"I could try."

"Then try. We can have that night and the next morning. Then I'll race while you—I don't know— maybe you can find a garage sale or two around here."

She laughed. "Now you're getting the idea. Okay, I'll see what I can do. I have a new plan for work, too, of delegating more responsibility. This fits right in."

"I love you so much. I don't know how I'll wait until then."

She cradled the phone against her cheek. "Me neither."

"Let me come down tonight."

"No. My house is still crowded, as you once so aptly described it. This plan is better."

He groaned. "Okay. Expect me to call you every night this week. And now I'd better hang up, before I head down there whether you like it or not."

"Good night, my love." Smiling, Lila replaced the receiver. She was in love—with herself, with Bill and with the future.

LILA ORCHESTRATED her business operations so that she left town right after work the evening of December thirtieth. Traffic was terrible, but she was too excited to care. She'd left the house to the girls, who had found a babysitter for New Year's Eve and had decided to take Mike to the party. Mike had called often during the past week, and between his calls and Bill's, and Penny's reports on the progress of her wedding plans, Lila's telephone line was seldom free.

Penny had been ecstatic that Lila was going up to stay with Bill, and she'd already offered to forestall her wedding date in case there was a chance of making it a double ceremony. Lila had told her not to count on anything so immediate.

She pulled into Bill's driveway and the garage door slid up. She saw him standing inside the lighted interior waiting for her, and she almost stalled the car in her excitement. He punched the control to close the door and came toward her car, his smile wider than she'd ever seen it, even when he'd just won a race. She scrambled out of the driver's seat and into his arms.

"I thought you'd never get here." He kissed her hungrily and slipped his hands beneath her coat to bring her as close as possible. "Have you had dinner?" he murmured, nuzzling her throat.

"No, but it doesn't matter."

"That's all the answer I need. Come in the house. We'll worry about your stuff later."

They ran up the stairs holding hands and tumbled onto the bed, all the while unbuttoning, unfastening, pushing aside the impediments to their union.

When at last they became one, Bill gazed into Lila's eyes. "We belong together," he said. "Forever."

"Yes," she agreed, bringing his head down for a kiss. "Yes."

THEY DEVOTED THE NIGHT to the glorious reunion of their bodies, which seemed created to give pleasure to each other. Serious discussion, they both agreed, could wait for morning, after they'd had a chance to slake their thirst for making love.

Finally, over breakfast the next morning, Bill proposed a walk. "It's the safest way to keep me on the topic of our future," he said. "I'll have a little more trouble seducing you on a suburban street. And I definitely have things I want to say. It's just that your mouth keeps getting in the way and I end up kissing you, instead."

Lila chuckled and put on her jacket. "Would you rather I walked down to the corner and called you from a pay phone?"

"Don't be a smarty-pants." He zipped up his windbreaker and led her into the fog-enshrouded morning. "You should feel right at home in this," he commented, taking her hand.

"Right. I'll pretend the traffic on the main road is the surf."

"Well, it's a temporary fantasy you'll have to create. I've decided that your need for the ocean is greater than my reluctance to live in the dampness. If you'll have me, I'd like to move in with you."

She stopped in the middle of the sidewalk. "What?"

"My goodness," he said, turning to face her. "You look totally surprised."

"I am totally surprised."

"Then you don't understand how desperately I need you," he said softly, touching her cheek. "Once you told me you'd cut the girls loose, I began rethinking everything. You're right. I can rebuild my business down there, and if the ocean means so much to you, I can adjust. It's a small price to pay."

She gazed up at him, unable to comprehend that he'd willingly sacrifice so much for her. But the light in his eyes told her that he meant every word. "I love you so much," she whispered.

"Careful. You're liable to touch off a chain reaction, looking at me that way."

"Bill, you're wonderful to suggest this plan."

"Not wonderful, just lecherously inclined toward a certain voluptuous brunette. Ready to go back to the house, now that we have that settled? I don't have to leave for the track until eleven o'clock."

Lila took a deep breath. "I think we'd better walk some more," she said, squeezing his hand.

"Oh? Have I lost my appeal already?"

"No way. But I have some things to say, too."

"Okay."

They walked along the misty street while Lila phrased and rephrased her arguments in her mind. Perhaps she was a fool. After all, he'd offered to give up everything for her. Penny would probably tell her to take it and shut up.

"This is driving me crazy, Lila. What is it? After last night, I can't believe you've changed your mind, or that there's someone else, but if you have bad news, let's get it out in the open, and fast."

"Nothing like that, Bill."

"We don't even have to make it legal, if that's what's bothering you. Although I had really hoped that you'd want to be my wife as much as I want to be your husband."

"I do. I do want to be your wife. But I don't think either of us should rip up the lives we've built for ourselves in the process."

"I don't look at it that way. But you obviously do, so I'll make the changes. It's okay, Lila."

"No, it's not okay." His hand tensed in hers but she plunged on. "Look, we love each other now as we are. I don't know what might happen to our love if we start making drastic changes. I wonder if you'd start resenting being forced to live in a place you wouldn't have ordinarily chosen. What happens if the business doesn't grow fast enough to satisfy you? What happens when you get sick to death of having two cats around all the time?"

He glanced at her. "Who told you I didn't like cats?"

"I guessed."

"Lila, surely we're not going to allow a couple of cats to—"

"Cats aren't really the issue. Individuality is. I don't think you should twist yourself into a shape that suits me, and I shouldn't do that for you, either."

"Wait." He swung her around by the shoulders. "This is sounding dangerously like a no-win situation. I love you, woman, and I'll do what has to be done so that I can be with you. I can't make myself plainer than that."

"I can't ask you to make the sacrifice.

"Does that mean you're going to refuse it?"

"Yes, but—"

He gripped her shoulders. "Lila, please," he said, his voice low. "Please don't make me beg."

Her heart thumped rapidly. "Give me a chance to explain," she said. "This may sound crazy, but I think we could be married and each still live in our own houses."

The agony in his eyes slowly gave way to disbelief. "What the hell good is that?"

"Lots of good," she pleaded. "We'll trade off on weekends, maybe even work our businesses so we have three-day weekends more often. Since we're both self-employed, we ought to be able to manage that."

"And what about the rest of the days? What about eating alone, and sleeping alone and missing—"

"Is there a chance that we'd appreciate each other more, that we'd cherish the time we had together because we didn't take it for granted?"

"I can't imagine ever taking you for granted, and if I'm privileged to live with you for the rest of my life, it won't be long enough. I'll never have enough time to talk with you, laugh with you, touch you. How can you think of chopping off half of that available time?"

Lila's stomach churned. This response was the one she'd feared. She still had time to take back everything she'd said, to admit the idea was ridiculous and that of course they'd get along fine after he moved to La Jolla. But she didn't think they would. The magical connection between them could so easily become prisoners' shackles.

"Maybe," Bill continued, releasing his grip on her shoulders, "maybe this is your way of saying you don't love me enough."

"No! This is my way of saying I love you too much to change you!" Tears gathered in her eyes. He didn't understand.

"Maybe we'd better go back. I have to get ready for the race." His expression closed off, and he started back down the sidewalk.

She hurried after him. "Please give this idea a chance, Bill. Please think about it, and please know that I love you."

"I'm having a hard time believing it. Here I throw myself at your feet, offer to do whatever you want, and you tell me to stay in my little corner of the world."

"That's not how I meant it," Lila said, miserable. "I'm only trying to preserve what's unique about each of us, to protect—"

"To protect yourself, I guess. I never felt I needed to be protected from you."

They walked rapidly and soon reached the house. Lila followed Bill upstairs to the bedroom. "I'm not leaving, Bill. I'll be here when you get back."

"Suit yourself. I wouldn't want to cramp your style by telling you what to do."

"Bill, you're being unreasonable!"

He whirled around to face her. "*I'm* being unreasonable? That's a good one. Correct me if I'm wrong, but I seem to remember a discussion in which you got upset because I wouldn't consider living with you in La Jolla. Now I offer to do that, and you reject the idea. Who's unreasonable, Lila?"

She swallowed. "You're right. I did say those things before, but I hadn't thought things through."

"And now you have?"

"Yes."

"Pardon me if I don't leap on this new bandwagon of yours. For all I know, I'll agree to this idea and you'll tell me that you've reconsidered that, too."

"That's not fair. You caught me by surprise with the ring, and the proposal. I spoke off the top of my head, exactly the way, I might add, you're doing now."

"Is that so? Well, whatever I'm speaking off of is about to stop. I have a race to run." He pulled open a dresser drawer and began rummaging through it.

"I'm going with you."

"That's dumb. You've already told me you don't like watching me race."

"I don't, but I can't let you go off alone. You're upset. You might—"

"Crash?" He leveled a piercing look at her. "Let me put your mind to rest. When I'm on that track, I concentrate on racing, period. I won't drive any differently today than I ever do."

"Nevertheless, I'm going."

He shrugged. "Suit yourself," he said again.

Half an hour later they drove to the track in silence. Lila had run out of arguments, and Bill didn't seem to be in the mood for further discussion. She tried to convince herself that he'd be all right in the race today, but whenever she glanced at the tense set of his jaw, she doubted it.

Jack and Raphael greeted her enthusiastically, but Raphael soon picked up on Bill's tension. When Bill went to buy soft drinks for everyone and Jack was busy under the hood, Raphael quietly asked Lila what was going on.

"I've hurt his feelings," she said. "He was willing to sell his business and move to La Jolla, and I told him not to, that I thought we could be married and each still continue in our own houses. He thinks . . . that I can't love him very much if I want that. But Raphael, I suggested it *because* I love him. I want him to be where he's happy, and that's not in La Jolla."

Raphael studied her for a moment. "When my wife stopped coming to the racetrack, I thought she didn't love me very much, either. Finally, I figured out that if she didn't love me, she'd have asked me to give it up and spend the time with her, instead."

"How long before you had that insight?"

"Months."

Lila groaned.

"But I wasn't very smart," Raphael added, "Maybe Bill's smarter than me."

"Raphael, I'm scared silly about him going out on the track today. You've seen how he's behaving. Isn't it dangerous?"

"Maybe, but I'd guess not. He might drive more aggressively than usual, but he's not foolish, like some of the young kids. That's the thing about Bill. He's not out there only for personal glory. He thinks of the safety of the other drivers, too. It'd be nice if all the guys were that way."

"You're right. He's really special, Raphael. I just wish—"

"Here he comes," Raphael warned. "Hang tough, Lila. And don't give up."

Lila knew she couldn't give up. That was why she'd come to the race today, even though she hadn't wanted to. She really couldn't blame Bill for reacting the way he had; her response could have seemed like a rejection.

As the time drew near for Bill's race, she paced around the infield and reminded herself of all that Raphael had said about Bill's maturity behind the wheel. When she noticed him zipping up his suit, she approached tentatively, not knowing if he'd want his good-luck kiss or not.

They gazed at each other, and finally he muttered an oath and swept her into his arms. His kiss was rough and angry. Then he released her and pulled on his face protector without saying a word. She quaked with fear as he pulled on his gloves and climbed in behind the wheel.

All through the pace lap she prayed for him to stay safe. The outcome of their relationship didn't matter at this moment. All she wanted was to have him cross the finish line in one piece. Her usual method for enduring the races had been to distract herself by talking with other people in the pit area, but today she followed every movement of Bill's yellow car. She roamed the infield as the pack of cars approached the starting line and picked up speed.

Once across the line, Bill shot out in front. Lila dug her fingernails into her palms as she followed his progress around the track. No one seemed able to catch him until a red Corvette driving recklessly careened around several cars and challenged Bill.

Raphael came to stand beside Lila. "That kid is the kind I was talking about," he said above the roar of the engines. "No sense. Look at him."

Lila wanted to close her eyes as the red car threatened to ram Bill several times in the process of trying to pass, but Bill managed to evade the younger driver and keep the lead. Still, the red car kept coming, and as the last lap began, the driver veered left and right, risking a flip in order to pass Bill.

"That guy's nuts!" Jack yelled, running over to Lila and Raphael. "He doesn't seem to care what happens to him or his car."

Like a rabbit transfixed by headlights, Lila moved around the infield to keep track of the battle between Bill and the red car. On the far turn she heard the roar when the red car surged forward and there seemed nowhere for it to go. If Bill held his position, they'd crash. Lila watched, horrified, her whole body braced for the impact.

It never came. Bill dropped back and gave the red car the lead. Lila sagged as the tension left her in a rush and tears welled in her eyes. Raphael had been right. Bill wouldn't take unnecessary risks just to win. Until now, she hadn't really believed it, but seeing this race would reduce a great many of her fears, and for that alone, she was grateful.

When Bill wheeled into the pit, Jack and Raphael rushed forward, incensed at the behavior of the winning driver. As they ranted about poor sportsmanship, he tugged off his face protector and grinned at them. "Lighten up. He's just a kid."

Lila's heart warmed with love. She longed to run to him, but she hesitated. There had been fury in his last kiss, despite the fact he'd claimed it. So she waited several yards away.

Bill unzipped his suit and glanced around. When he saw her, he started toward her with a deliberate stride. *This is it*, she thought, knowing from the determination on his face that he'd made a decision about their future. She couldn't tell from his expression what that decision was.

He stopped in front of her. "This isn't easy," he began.

Lila closed her eyes. It was over.

"You were right about my moving permanently to La Jolla. It would never work."

She opened her eyes and blinked back the tears.

"I realized that while I was driving."

"I thought you always concentrated on driving, period," she said.

"Usually I do. Except when a certain brunette is on my mind."

She gasped. "Bill, you shouldn't have driven. I told you it was dangerous. Don't you realize that anything could have happened?"

"Maybe, and maybe I got lucky. But I'm glad I raced. Ideas came to me so fast, as if my brain had become a pressure cooker."

"What—what ideas?" she ventured.

"I thought of you out there, not wanting to be, enduring for my sake. I hated that. Then immediately I realized that's what you were afraid would happen to me in La Jolla, that I'd endure, miserably, for your sake. Am I right?"

Lila nodded.

He wiped the sweat from his forehead. "Well, thinking about the person you love as 'enduring' for your sake.... I discovered it's a lousy feeling."

"Yes." She still had no clue where the discussion was headed.

"We don't want lousy feelings ruining our marriage."

She stared at him, thoroughly confused.

"Dammit, woman, say something! Will you marry me or not?"

She caught her breath. "Marry you? You still—"

"You'd better believe I still—even if it has to be part-time," he said with a half smile.

She stood transfixed, not believing that her world, so recently upended, could so quickly be set right again.

Bill shook his head. "Lady, you would never make it as a race driver. You have no ability to make quick adjustments. But I'll ask you one more time. Are you willing to gamble on an old Billy-goat?"

She hurled herself into his arms. "Yes!" she cried. "Yes, yes, yes, yes, yes!"

He smiled into her upturned face. "You know, I think this beats a first-place trophy."

"It darn well better."

He lowered his lips to hers. "It does," he murmured. "Every time." Then he gently claimed his prize.

Everyone loves a spring wedding, and this April, Harlequin cordially invites you to read the most romantic wedding book of the year.

ONE WEDDING—FOUR LOVE STORIES FROM OUR MOST DISTINGUISHED HARLEQUIN AUTHORS:

BETHANY CAMPBELL
BARBARA DELINSKY
BOBBY HUTCHINSON
ANN McALLISTER

The church is booked, the reception arranged and the invitations mailed. All Diane Bauer and Nick Granatelli have to do is walk down the aisle. Little do they realize that the most cherished day of their lives will spark so many romantic notions....

Available wherever Harlequin books are sold.

Take 4 bestselling love stories FREE

Plus get a FREE surprise gift!